Beyond Pulp Reprints

A series of collections of stories by
(mostly) women who wrote for pulp science-fiction
and horror magazines of the 1920s-50s.

FETTERED

AND OTHER TALES OF TERROR

GREYE LA SPINA

edited by Michael W. Phillips Jr.

Book design and layout by Michael W. Phillips Jr.

Published by From Beyond Press | Chicago, IL
frombeyondpress.com
mike@frombeyondpress
Instagram & Twitter: @frombeyondpress

ISBN: 979-8-9875743-3-1
LCCN: 2023947520

Contents

Introduction vii

On Scaring Oneself into Conniptions 1

The Last Cigarette 5

The Remorse of Professor Panebianco 9

The Scarf of the Beloved 19

Wolf of the Steppes 25

Fettered... 49

Introduction

Michael W. Phillips Jr.

At the age of 38, Greye La Spina decided that it was time to become a prolific and beloved writer. She had already experienced marriage, motherhood, and widowhood, but she threw herself into her new career, publishing more than one hundred stories, serials, and plays in a variety of magazines over the next thirty-two years. She was especially prominent in weird fiction, where she enjoyed financial, critical, and popular success as a favorite writer for *The Thrill Book* and *Weird Tales*. And then, like many women who wrote for the pulps, she was forgotten. I hope that this book plays a part in bringing her, and her contemporaries, back into the conversation about the roots of horror fiction.

BECOMING GREYE LA SPINA

La Spina was born Fanny Greye Bragg on July 10, 1880 in Wakefield, Massachusetts to 28-year-old Ella Celia (Perkins) Bragg and her husband Lorenzo Dow Bragg, a 70-year-old retired Methodist clergyman who had ridden circuit in Texas before the Civil War. Greye was one of five children, only two of whom lived past childhood.[1]

She was a writer from an early age. As an elementary school student, she published a neighborhood newspaper in Bridgeport, CT, that "sold to neighbors for 15 common pins," and in high school,

---

1. I gathered biographical details from a variety of sources including online ancestry sites.

she won a *Connecticut Magazine* writing contest with an essay about Major General Israel Putnam, a Revolutionary War hero.[2]

On June 5, 1899, shortly before her nineteenth birthday, she married Ralph Emil Geissler. She gave birth to a daughter, Celia, on August 29, 1900. Less than a year later, on April 4, 1901, Ralph died, and she embarked on a new career as a working widowed mother. She remarried in 1910, this time to Rosario Robert La Spina, a deposed Italian baron. She worked as likely the first woman newspaper photographer in New York, and also worked as a stenographer and office manager for a while. She wrote a little—the August 1915 issue of *McCall's* contains her article about crocheting Venetian lace, a favorite pastime of hers—and she raised her daughter.

"BY NATURE AN INVETERATE EXPERIMENTER": A WRITING LIFE

Having successfully shepherded her daughter to adulthood, La Spina tells us, "in 1918 I decided that it was time to start a new profession, writing." She had been interested in the occult from a young age, and she threw herself into her research; a 1946 newspaper profile describes her "pointing round the room where the bookshelves groaned with volumes of lore." She put that research to work on her first story: "So one evening I typed out a rough draft of 'Wolf of the Steppes,' scaring myself to such an extent that I turned on all the lights when I finished it and retired at 2:00 AM."[3]

That brilliant werewolf story (reprinted in this volume) was chosen as the cover story for the first issue of *The Thrill Book*, itself groundbreaking as the first magazine to prioritize horror, fantasy, and science fiction. She published at least six stories in the two-year run of the magazine, several of them under pseudonyms such as

---

2. Robert Weinberg, *The Weird Tales Story* (Fax Collector's Editions, 1977), pp. 49-50.

3. Quoted in Weinberg, p. 50; "Greye La Spina, Weaves Weird Tales and Tapestries, Finds Life Is 'Fun' Amidst Solitudes of Spinnerstown." Allentown (PA) Sunday *Call-Chronicle*, March 10, 1946, newspapers.com/article/18765514/greye_la_spina_weaves_weird_tales/.

Isra Putnam and Ezra Putnam, drawn from that high-school essay about General Putnam. For other magazines, she wrote as the Baroness di Savuto, which would have been her title had her husband's family retained their Italian barony.

She told Robert Weinberg that writing came easy to her. "I had great fun writing all kinds of fiction and selling it easily; it never occurred to me that writers could have trouble selling their yarns!" Although it's often stated that she published over one hundred stories and serials, it's unclear where that number comes from. We know for sure of around fifty, and given the sorry state of preservation of magazines published in the early decades of the twentieth century, it's easy to accept that fifty more stories have yet to be rediscovered or have disappeared forever, crumbled to dust.[4]

The sheer variety of her oeuvre is staggering. She told readers of *Weird Tales* in March 1942 that "I am by nature an inveterate experimenter," and it shows. In addition to scary stories for a variety of outlets, she wrote for two-fisted men's magazines like *Action Stories* and the teen-oriented adventure pulp *Top-Notch Magazine*; mildly titillating women's magazines like *Saucy Stories* and *Parisienne Monthly* (both founded by H.L. Mencken to fund his more literary pursuits); detective magazines including *Black Mask* and *Bull's-Eye Detective*; more serious women's magazines like *Metropolitan*; and, likely, magazines we'll never know about. For example, she mentions in that 1946 newspaper interview that she wrote "sophisticated Italian stories—little sweet homey stories of Italians in America," but none of her known stories would seem to fit that description. She was as good as she was prolific, too: in 1925, she won a $2500 second prize in a short-story contest sponsored by *Photoplay Magazine* for her story "A Seat at the Table," a touching tale of a poor pastor attending a college reunion. (First prize went to Octavus Roy Cohen, who wrote incredibly racist comedies, and third went to Adela Rogers St. Johns, the most famous woman journalist of the first half of the twentieth century.)[5]

---

4. For an exhaustive list of the stories we know about, see The FictionMags Index, philsp.com/homeville/fmi/n05/n05361.htm#A53

5. "Greye La Spina, Weaves Weird Tales"; *The Writer's Digest*, March 1922,

"GEMS OF SINISTER MENACE": WEIRD TALES

Over the course of 27 years, La Spina published seventeen stories and serials in *Weird Tales*—a magazine that, at least at first, needed her as much as she needed it. Eric Leif Davin, in *Partners in Wonder: Women and the Birth of Science Fiction, 1926-1965*, says "early female authors like Greye La Spina, who already had a track record in earlier pulp magazines…brought needed cachet to the venture." And Davin quotes legendary editor Donald A. Wollheim, who wrote, "Greye La Spina is one of the original group of *Weird Tales* writers whose stories helped a good deal to establish that oldest existing fantasy magazine in its formative days of 1923 and 1924."[6]

Not only was she important to the early success of *Weird Tales*, she was also the fifth most published woman after Allison V. Harding, Mary Elizabeth Counselman, G.G. Pendarves, and Everil Worrill. Praise for her stories filled "The Eyrie," the letters column of *Weird Tales*. Sci-fi writer Arthur J. Burks wrote, "I never believed I would like stories written by a woman…I am convinced! I am humbled in the very dirt! I am no longer an egoist!" August Derleth, who later would publish her only standalone novel, wrote, "Greye La Spina's stories are gems of sinister menace." Readers regularly named her stories as their favorites, listing her alongside H.P. Lovecraft, Seabury Quinn, and Frank Belknap Long as masters of horror fiction. Davin notes that "some of the highest reader-voted stories in the entire existence of *Weird Tales* were by female authors [including] Greye La Spina."[7]

When she was absent from the magazine for any length of time, readers noticed. After a gap of some three years between stories, Roy Roland, of Detroit, asked in 1930, "What has happened to Greye La Spina? If it is at all possible, let us have a story by this interesting writer of ghost tales. I believe it is about three years since

---

p. 29.
6. Eric Leif Davin, *Partners in Wonder: Women and the Birth of Science Fiction, 1926-1965* (Lexington Books, 2006), p. 66.
7. Arthur J. Burks, "The Eyrie," *Weird Tales*, November 1925; August Derleth, "The Eyrie," *Weird Tales*, February 1926; Davin, p. 67.

x

he has appeared within the pages of W.T." (La Spina was often mistaken for a man.) In 1942, after an eight-year absence while she was running a farm and taking care of her sick husband in rural Pennsylvania, a fan named L.L. Mockler wrote, "It was nice to see that Greye La Spina had come out from obscurity on a farm to give us one of her stories. Here's hoping to see more of her work."[8]

"WHAT HAS HAPPENED TO GREYE LA SPINA?"

Why, then, is she mostly forgotten today? She published her last story in 1951, and except for Arkham House's 1960 publication of her 1925 serial novel *Invaders from the Dark* (which *Weird Tales* readers had praised as "greater than *Dracula*"), she was mostly out of print. No collections of her shorter works appeared in the 1960s when a younger generation of writers was discovering their pulp horror progenitors. Only a handful of her stories were reprinted in the United States between 1960 and the 1990s. Robert Weinberg, who perhaps did more in his life to resurrect the reputation of pulp writers than anyone else aside from August Derleth, published a chapbook in 1972 containing two of her stories, but only 500 copies were printed. She fared a bit better in the UK, but essentially, she disappeared.[9]

It's possible that it had something to do with H.P. Lovecraft's disdain for her. The prolific correspondent disparaged her in letters to fellow writers Natalie H. Wooley ("Mrs. La Spina is distinctly mediocre—full of clichés and cheap romantic devices."), Clark Ashton Smith ("The La Spina novelette somehow drags along very dully—with triteness & triviality sapping at what might be suspensefully horrible."), and her future editor August Derleth ("the La Spina thing left me cold even though I recognised a fine chance for horrific atmosphere"). Perhaps this disdain was passed on to his acolytes

---

8. Roy Roland, "The Eyrie," *Weird Tales*, October 1930; L.L. Mocker, "The Eyrie," *Weird Tales*, July 1942.
9. Greye La Spina, *The Gargoyle: A Tale of Devil Worship* (Robert Weinberg, 1972) also contained "The Devil's Pool."

and the bibliographers who have devoted their lives to him.[10]

When she wasn't being ignored, she was being minimized. Lee Server's entry about her in his *Encyclopedia of Pulp Fiction Writers* (2002) at times reads like a checklist of the methods Joanna Russ outlined in *How to Suppress Women's Writing* (1983), opening with "La Spina's significance is more historical than artistic," and continuing with factual errors and dismissive statements. A few critics have published glowing appraisals of her work, including Mike Barrett, who wrote, "Although virtually forgotten, Greye La Spina made lasting contributions to the annals of weird fiction, and her status in the field has been underestimated and overlooked for many years."[11]

"INTERESTING STORIES IN INTERESTING WAYS": A REAPPRAISAL

Looking at La Spina's biography and bibliography, I'm reminded of the idea that Ginger Rogers did everything that Fred Astaire did, but backward and in high heels. As interesting as her life was, as many stories as she published, La Spina was nonetheless a woman and a mother in the early decades of the twentieth century. Thus, her writing career began only after she had finished raising a child as a working single mother, and it faltered when her second husband became ill and she had to care for him and the family farm. Imagine the heights she might have reached had she been able to devote more of her time to writing. Read the brilliant *Invaders from the Dark* and *Fettered* and imagine the novels she didn't have time to write.

The thing that stands out to me is the quality of the stories. Yes, they're breathless and overwrought in that charming early pulp manner, but they breeze by instead of plodding along, weighed down by a thesaurus chained around their necks (looking at you,

----

10. Bobby Derie, Deep Cuts in a Lovecraftian Vein, "The Devil's Pool" (1932) by Greye La Spina, April 20, 2022. deepcuts.blog/2022/04/20/the-devils-pool-1932-by-greye-la-spina

11. Lee Server, *Encyclopedia of Pulp Fiction Writers* (Facts on File, 2002); Mike Barrett, "Weaver of Weird Tales: Greye La Spina," in *Doors to Elsewhere* (Alchemy Press, 2013), pp. 45-61.

HPL). She thought a lot about structure, and she outlined her approach to Weinberg: she must "produce first of all an atmosphere of mounting apprehension, subtly rising in its suspense. This must become so powerful that my readers must be gripped by it sufficiently to read on to the climax." It worked: Seabury Quinn complained to "The Eyrie" that he had missed his subway stop because he was so engrossed in the conclusion of *Invaders from the Dark*. Mike Barrett says, "The verve of the narratives and their created moods make the tales memorable in their own right. Ultimately they preserve their ability to entertain not simply because they are period pieces, but because they tell interesting stories in interesting ways and, most important of all, they are thoroughly enjoyable."[12]

In addition to being very good, they're different from those of her male contemporaries, a reflection of La Spina's unique life and her status as a woman writing in a field dominated by men. (This is not to say that she was unique *because* she was a woman—almost a fifth of the stories published in *Weird Tales* were by women.) She plays with typical horror tropes—vampires, werewolves, mad scientists—but her takes are wholly original. Barrett says of these stories, "each covered standard themes but in more imaginative ways than the fiction of many of her contemporaries…When vampires do appear, as in the serial *Fettered*, the story progresses in a far from orthodox manner." Modern werewolf mythology had not crystallized when she wrote "Wolf of the Steppes," and so her account of how werewolves are created is fresh and unique, but was nonetheless informed by La Spina's thorough research in the occult. Her mad scientist story "The Remorse of Professor Panebianco" (Professor Whitebread!) boils down to a tale of a man who's too busy mad-sciencing to realize that his wife wants to have sex. *Fettered* features a vampire woman who becomes much more hot and bothered over the young woman protagonist than over her dunderheaded brother. These stories are different: partly because La Spina was a woman, partly because she lived a remarkable life, mostly because she was

---

12. Greye La Spina, "The Eyrie," *Weird Tales*, March 1942; Quinn quoted in Weinberg, p. 25; Barrett, p. 46.

a remarkable writer.

Perhaps now is her time. The 100th anniversary of the first issue of *Weird Tales* has prompted increased interest in the women who wrote weird fiction, and in 2020 she took her place alongside her contemporaries Everil Worrill, Eli Colter, and Mary Elizabeth Counselman in Valancourt Books' *The Women of Weird Tales*. The volume you hold in your hands is the first major collection of her work, but there are so many stories I couldn't include, and so many that remain to be rediscovered, that I doubt it will be the last.

IN THIS VOLUME

This book contains five pieces by La Spina. The delightful essay "On Scaring Oneself into Conniptions" draws the curtain back on the process of writing weird tales. "The Last Cigarette" is a revenge tale with an O. Henry twist, and "The Remorse of Professor Panebianco" turns the mad scientist genre on its head. The ethereal mood piece "The Scarf of the Beloved" recalls Edgar Allan Poe. Her epistolary masterpiece "Wolf of the Steppes" is a werewolf story unlike anything you've ever read. Finally, her short novel *Fettered* takes the vampire myth in surprising directions.

ACKNOWLEDGEMENTS

This book would not exist without archivists and librarians, especially the ones at the Internet Archive, the Interlibrary Loan department at the University of Chicago Library, and Special Collections at the University of California-Davis Library. I owe a great debt to Robert Weinberg and Mike Barrett, but any mistakes are mine. This book is dedicated to the late Professor Carol Green-Ramirez, who taught me how to write, to think critically, to become a feminist, and to find things out. I hope that if you were still around, you'd give a slight nod and say, "Not bad, Mike."

On Scaring Oneself into Conniptions

Science-Fantasy Correspondent,
January-February 1937

Writer's cramp? One hears little of that nowadays. Writer's thrills? What in the world are they? Almost any seasoned writer will warn the amateur never to write with tongue in cheek. Editors and readers are bound to sense any insincerity in work produced by a writer who is secretly sneering at his own products. Being too honest and sincere while producing occult and supernatural material, however, is not always conducive to a writer's peace of mind; even if the editor and reader get a big thrill out of the yarn, the wretched writer is apt to scare himself almost to death while writing it if he too closely follows the suggested procedure. Yet, like a drug addict, he will continue to produce weird stories, more perhaps for himself than for his public. For he gets such a thrill out of them himself that he cannot let them alone.

The first story I ever wrote for publication (it was featured in the now defunct *Thrill Book* of Street & Smith) was called "Wolf of the Steppes." It was a grrrrand werewolf story, believe me! Before writing it, I steeped myself in werewolf and other supernatural lore as well as in certain mystical branches of mental science, and I worked out such a logical argument for werewolf existence that I could not persuade myself nightly that I would not meet one at the head of the staircase or have one snapping at my heels when I made the fearsome dash upward in the wee small hours.

My family (how admirable of them!) believed that I could do anything I set out to accomplish. When I announced that I had decided to be an author, they fixed me up a corner of the dining-room for a studio. This corner, where I sat with my back to the wall (a wise procedure when writing scary yarns), was shut in by a tall four-leafed screen. As I was busy in an office during the day, writing had to be done at night, usually after the family had retired in awe-stricken respect. A swinging door between kitchen and dining-room became my bête-noir. There were breathless, horrifying moments when a vagrant breeze would push against it hard enough to move it with reluctant creaks. At such times I would freeze in my chair, hardly daring to breathe; my eyes would go cautiously to that screen, and I would momentarily expect a gaunt, hairy visage to peer malevolently down at me over its tall top. My heart would be in my throat; my stomach would be a sickening vacuum; my hair would bristle on my head. When the door would stop creaking, I would draw a long breath and very cautiously begin once more to type, still with an occasional glance at the screen.

The difficult time was when drowsiness would overcome my tired lids and I knew that I must brave the world beyond my shielding screen—the dark, creepy, shuddery world of vampires, werewolves, and ghostly visitants from the nether regions. Cautiously drawing the screen aside, I would peer into the shadowy room before venturing forth to snap on a light that sent the threatening shades scuttling into the shelter of the black hallway. Then, and not until then, was the "studio" light snapped off. Thus by degrees did I make my shivering progress from the dining-room to the hall, from the hall to the foot of the stairs—and back again to snap off the lower light after the upper one had been put on, as there was no two-way switch in that house. Even with that upper light, the lower part of the staircase was steeped in ominous darkness. A werewolf might easily have thrust its sharp-nailed claws through the banisters! A werewolf might easily have bounded up behind those fleeing ankles, with snapping, slathering jaws! Ugh! How the backbone did prickle and tingle!

To this very day I almost scare myself to death when I write a weird tale. When I'm writing it, I believe it's true. I've had folks ask me whether I really believed in werewolves. I cannot give them an unequivocal yes or no, because it all depends on circumstances. If it's broad daylight and I'm writing something s s & g [sweet, simple, and girlish], I shake my head and smile significantly. But if it's night-time, if I'm mulling over a weird story, or in the throes of writing one! Ah, then I must reply, "Werewolves are real! Vampires exist! Ghosts walk the haunted earth!"

For the writer of the occult gets far more thrills out of producing his work than an editor or reader can get from manuscript or published magazine. And, like a drug addict, the writer of weird fiction goes back always in his hunger for the thrills only his own creative art can give him…and produces another weird tale.

The Last Cigarette

Weird Tales, March 1925

Milton Wheeler's thickset body shivered as he put a match to the wick of the oil heater, noting mechanically that the reservoir was almost empty. Before he could get more oil, he would have to settle that already large bill owing the grocer.

He paced the floor to stir his torpid circulation, rubbing his stubby hands together briskly.

His gray suit was much too light for November, and his undergarments—repeatedly darned and patched by Agnes' hands—too thin to yield their original warmth. He owed the tailor for that new black overcoat; as for the underwear, he would first have to pay for last summer's things and for the new black hat, before ordering other garments. A black suit he had not quite dared to order. Not that the tailor had actually asked for money, but he had observed casually that he wouldn't send in his little bill until after the funeral.

After the funeral! Milton shivered again, this time with cold. Everything was coming in—after the funeral.

He felt that Agnes had dealt him almost a personal blow by dying; without her cooperation, how could he keep up with his pretenses? It would be a few days only, before his hated rival would learn upon how small a foundation had been built Milton's house of sham. That Benson, who had in everything but the winning of Agnes triumphed over him, should learn of his failure to make a success financially, was to Milton a frightful tragedy.

Milton had had a few thousand dollars in the bank, and a fair salary at the laboratory, when he married Agnes, winning her from Benson, who had large private means. (It was the first time since they two had been boys in school together that Milton had triumphed over the other man.) It had been indescribably galling to him to think that Benson would ever learn how much Agnes had lost in marrying a poorer man. Agnes had rebelled at this deception in the beginning; she did not care, she said. But then she saw how keenly Milton felt about it—how his every through was turned in the one direction. Poor girl! Her first unkind act had been her desertion of him at this critical moment.

Milton had managed to fool everybody. He had kept up a lavish establishment, spending his principal freely. He had bought Agnes everything that could make the impression of unlimited means upon the rejected Benson, whose keen eyes he fancied were always upon him. Agnes' death, however, found him penniless; without a position; confronting a mountain of unpaid bills. Rent, unsettled for four months; groceries, the sum was almost staggering; butcher, how could they have consumed such quantities of meat?

The doctor—somehow this account had mounted up to much more than Milton had anticipated. There must have been many visits to the office of which Agnes' husband was ignorant; she must have kept her sickness from him a much longer time than he had realized. To the doctor's statement Milton had pinned, with sardonic humor, bills from the druggist, the florist, the undertaker.

Then there were coal bills; laundry bills; ice bills. The sum of those items marshaled itself before him with malignant triumph, conveying to his shrinking spirit the overwhelming prevision of defeat.

Men were being turned away everywhere. He might be months finding another such position as he had been holding for four years. He might raise money to settle that appalling total of debt by paying the exorbitant interest rate of some loan shark, but even this would be only a temporary relief. Discovery of his castle of pretense was inevitable, and to him disclosure of the real facts meant such complete, such utter ruin, that the bare idea bowed him down into the very dust of humiliation. He could see Benson's smile . . .

There was only one way out. Death! It was distasteful to him, because his death under present circumstances would mean the disclosure of what he had for three years been struggling to conceal. His death, with the revelation of that appalling sum total of debt, would make him the subject of derision for his rival.

If there were only some way to escape without baring his sordid secret to the world! He whipped his dulled mind into unwilling concentration. And then—suddenly—he had it! Within the dusk the little heater cast a circle of friendly radiance. Milton threw a glance upward... The lamp hook in that great beam across the middle of the ceiling looked strong enough. In the laundry there was always plenty of good rope. He would bring up a stepladder...

Half an hour later he jimmied open from the outside one of the study windows giving on the garden; the gusty November air swirled into the room, setting the curtains a-flutter. Upon the floor under his writing desk he laid a ten-dollar bill as if it had been accidentally dropped by hurried fingers. The balance of his last week's salary he tore carefully into small pieces and burned, scattering the ashes on the night wind from the open window. He pulled out both desk drawers, tossing their contents upon table and floor as if some unlicensed intruder had gone through them hastily.

Upon the bronze tray of his desk he laid a sheet of paper, inscribed with a few terse, carefully thought out words. He had disposed of all his securities, he wrote, to charities in which he and his wife had been interested, but had left sufficient cash in the desk drawer to settle all outstanding accounts against his estate. He chuckled as he wrote, a humorless sound, and then, shrugging his thick shoulders, finished: "I cannot live without Agnes. I am going to join her."

In those last moments he was capping the edifice of sham with the most marvelous of cupolas; he was putting the finishing touch to a work which for three years had been the driving force of his life. From boyhood he had had the worst of it with Benson, always; now Benson would be unable to smile in that slow, exasperating way of his. No, Benson would be obliged to think of him with astonished admiration.

He felt malicious enjoyment as he surveyed the indications of burglary, and the note that so well covered the traces of his supposed wealth. The fools would believe he had killed himself out of grief at the loss of his wife; they would continue to admire and envy him—and his secret would remain undiscovered.

Everything was ready. He lighted a cigarette contentedly. When he had finished this last smoke, he would climb the ladder, adjust the rope…It would be the greatest triumph of his life, after all—this death. His only regret was that he could not be there to enjoy the effect of the stupendous climax.

His cigarette finished, he flung the butt away and mounted the ladder. He felt gingerly of the rope knotted about his neck, shuddering involuntarily. If it were not that by dying he was making his secret secure for all time—. After all, it was the only way.

Setting his teeth, he pushed against the ladder with both feet. It toppled to the floor with a crash.

As his body was whirled about by the tautening rope, a flare from the bronze tray on the desk caught Milton's eye.

In that last poignant moment he had the mortification of observing that the cigarette butt had fallen upon and ignited the suicide note, that curled—crisped—blackened to an indecipherable ash before his agonized eyes.

The Remorse of Professor Panebianco

Weird Tales, January 1925

"Cielo, what an enormous crystal globe, Filippo!" exclaimed Dottore Giuseppe del Giovine, regarding the great inverted glass bell that hung over the professor's dissecting table. "What's the idea of that?" he added curiously.

The professor's black eyes rested upon the globe with the fondness of a parent. He pushed the table more centrally under the opening at the bell's lower extremity, then pulled on a chain operating a valve at the top.

"The purpose of this globe is to win me such recognition from the world of science as no man has ever enjoyed and no man after me can ever emulate," he responded, with a kind of grim enthusiasm.

"But how?"

The doctor was intensely interested.

"You are aware that Elena and I have long experimented on animals, to ascertain if that thing men call the 'soul' is at all tangible? We have now arrived at a very advanced point in our studies, so advanced that we are at a dead stop because we cannot obtain the necessary subjects for our next experiment."

"One can always find mice—or cats—or monkeys," said the doctor.

The professor shook his head decidedly.

"Such animals are things of the past, *caro amico*. We have seen the soul of a drowning mouse emerge from its body, in a spiral coil of vapor that wreathed its way out of the water to lose itself in the etheric spaces that include all life. We have watched the soul of a dying ape emerge in one long rush of fine, impalpable, smokelike

9

cloud that wound upward to become invisible as it, too, amalgamated with the invisible forces of the universe about us."

"I myself once saw what I believe might have been the soul of a dying man, as it departed from his body," asseverated the doctor, musingly.

"Ah, if one could but detain that fine essence of immortality, what wonders could not one work in time? What mighty secrets would perhaps be discovered!"

"You understand, then, Giuseppe *mio*, what I await with anxiety? The subject for the most tremendous experiment of all! It is futile for me to attempt to make it upon one of the lower animals, since they do not possess the power of reason, and their souls would therefore be by far too tenuous for a successful experiment. I have been trying for months to obtain possession of the person of some criminal condemned to death, that I might subject him to my theory as his dying breath fled, bearing with it his soul—that about which all men theorize, but which none have yet seen or conceived of as have I."

"The idea is tremendous, Filippo. What have the authorities done about it?"

"They refuse to assist me. I cannot tell them all that I desire to do, naturally, or my rivals would try to get ahead of me. Their stupid, petty jealousy! *Quanto è terribile!*"

"Exactly what do you wish to do, and how is this bell to serve you?" inquired the doctor, a puzzled series of lines drawing across his forehead.

"I have observed, *caro mio*, that the vaporous soul of the lower animal is so much lighter than the ether around it that it withstands the pull of gravity and rises, swaying with whatever currents of air are in the atmosphere, always to a higher level, where it dissipates into invisibility.

"I have been trying to possess myself of a living human being whose life was useless to the world, that his death might be made of transcendent value through my scientific knowledge. I constructed this crystal bell for a wonderful and stupendous purpose. It is intended to hold the tenuous wraith of the subject of my experiment.

"The valve above, open at first, will permit the air to escape at the top of the bell as it becomes displaced by the ascending essence of the dying man's soul. Then, when I pull the chain, thereby closing the valve, the soul would be retained by its own volatile nature within the bell, being unable to seek a lower level."

"Filippo, you astound me!"

There was something more than astonishment in the doctor's face, however, as his eyes searched the countenance of the professor sharply.

"My idea is indeed awe-inspiring, *caro dottore*. Your wonder is very natural," said the professor graciously.

"It must be trying to have to wait so long for a suitable subject for your experiment," ventured the doctor, with a side glance.

"Ah, how I shall love and venerate that human being who furnishes me with such a subject!" cried the professor fervently.

A deep sigh followed closely upon his words. The curtain hanging before the doorway was pushed to one side, as Elena Panebianco walked slowly into the room.

"How you will gaze upon that imprisoned soul!" cried she, with a passionate intensity that startled the doctor anew, as he turned his regard from her husband to her. "If it were a soul that loved you, how happy it would be to know that your entire thoughts were centered upon it, within the crystal bell! To see your eyes always fixed upon it, as it floated there within!"

She leaned weakly against the dissecting table, and her great eyes, dark with melancholic emotion, stared wildly out of her thin, fever-flushed face.

"*Tu sai impossibile!*" cried the professor. "What tragic jealousy is yours, Elena! A jealousy of things that do not as yet exist!"

Elena did not reply. She loved too deeply, too passionately, too irrevocably. And the only return her husband made was to permit her assistance in his laboratory work. Her eager mind had flown apace with his; not that she loved the work for itself, but that she longed to gain his approbation. To him the alluring loveliness of her splendid body was as nothing to the beauty of the wonderful intellect that gradually unfolded in his behalf.

In private, Filippo complained to the doctor that his wife was too demonstrative. She thought nothing of distracting his attention from important experiments, with pouting lips clamoring for a kiss, and not until he had hastily brushed her lips with his would she return to her work.

"I am obliged to bribe the woman with kisses," cried the professor, despairingly.

Elena had gone so far as to affirm to her husband that she was even jealous of his research, his experiments. That was unwise. No woman can interfere between a man and his chosen life-work. Such things are, as D'Annunzio puts it, *"piu che l'amore"* (greater than love), and prove relentless Juggernauts to those who tactlessly disregard the greater claims.

"He is worn out," said Elena to the doctor. "He has flung himself into his work to such an extent that nothing exists for him but that. He studies all night. He works all day. I have to force him to stop long enough to eat sufficient to maintain life."

"Go on, Elena, go on! When my head swims, I tie cold wet towels about it. When my brain refuses to obey me, I concentrate with inconceivable force of will upon my goal. Oh, Giuseppe *mio*, my very existence is bound up in this last experiment, which, alas! I am unable to complete because the authorities will not permit me to make use of the death of some criminal—a death that must be entirely useless to the scientific world, through their blind stupidity."

The doctor shrugged, with a gesture of his slender brown hands. His eyes sought Elena's face. Since he had been away the Signora Panebianco had altered terribly. She looked too delicate; she had faded visibly. Hectic roses flamed in her cheeks. Her thin hands, too, had been too cold when she touched his in greeting. Her constant cough racked her slender body. It seemed to Giuseppe del Giovine that she had become almost transparent, so slender had she become from loss of flesh. As she went from the room slowly with a gesture of helplessness, he turned to the professor.

"Your wife is a very sick woman," he declared, abruptly.

"I suppose she must be," Filippo responded absently. "She's very nervous, I know. She disturbs me inexcusably with silly demands for kisses and caresses, actually weeping when she thinks I don't see her, because I refuse to humor her foolish whims. I've been obliged, more than once, to drive her away with cold looks and hard words, because she has tried to coax me to stop work, insisting upon my talking with her."

He began adjusting his apparatus with an abstracted air. It was as well that he did not see the expression of indignation and despair that flashed across the mobile face of the physician, who had long loved Elena in secret, but hopelessly, as he very well knew, because she was absolutely indifferent to anybody but her husband.

"Yes, Giuseppe, she interrupts my most particular experiments to caress me ardently, trying to bring my lips down on hers. Often I have reproved her severely for attempting to turn me aside from my life-work. The man whose intellect has driven him to enter the precincts of the great mystery cannot stop to dally with the folly of fools, and love is the greatest folly of all."

"Blind fool, you!" muttered the doctor under his breath. "Love is the very breath of life itself!"

"If Elena is to assist me in my last experiment, the greatest of all, I must get a subject soon, for she is wasting away fast. Oh yes, I have observed it. Death has his fingers at her throat."

His voice was the voice of the man of science: there was not the slightest intonation that might have indicated other than passing interest in the unhappy Elena.

"What I am afraid of," he resumed, "is that even a human being's spirit will not materialize properly within the bell, unless instructed previously. And how can I expect a criminal to lend himself voluntarily to an experiment that necessitates his death for its success? No, the fool would cling too closely to his miserable life, and might even refuse to listen when I tried to prepare and instruct him. I ought to have for my experiment someone who knows just what I want done: someone who will carry out my wishes faithfully. And where am I to find such a person?" he finished lugubriously.

The curtains over the doorway swayed to admit Elena. It was only too evident from her expression that she had heard part, if not all. of her husband's words. There was an incomprehensible expression within those dark orbs that shrank not from the glance the professor turned upon the intruder.

"There is but one person in the whole world who could, and would, be able to carry out your ideas," said she, deliberately.

Filippo whirled upon Dottore del Giovine, relief and joy flashing over his face. Del Giovine gave a short exclamation and took an involuntary step forward, horror written on his face. The other man turned to Elena, caught her hands in his, and gazed down into those pellucid depths whence came the glow of a fire that burned within her heart for him alone.

"Elena! Can you really mean it? You fill me with the most intense, most vivid gratitude and admiration—and," he added hastily as if with an afterthought, "love."

"My life is burning low," was her quiet reply. "If my death can profit you, it is yours for the asking—if you desire it."

Stiff with incredulous horror, the doctor stood rooted to the spot. Elena knew what the professor desired; she was ready, willing, to serve as the subject of his experiment. It was for her a final proof of her love for him—and a test of his love for her. She realized that she alone, of all the world, knew the occult foundations of the science that would enable her to carry out successfully the other part of the experiment.

With an access of lofty emotions, Filippo Panebianeo gathered her into his arms and kissed her pallid brow. Elena's dark eyes closed ecstatically under this caress; she felt his heart beating high, but knew, alas! it was not for her; it was with renewed hope for the success of the stupendous performance to which he had long been irrevocably pledged.

"Now I shall vindicate myself to those who have called me a visionary, a madman!" Filippo cried in triumph.

His wife clung to him, her eyes seeking his with an appeal that he deliberately refused to recognize. He was only too afraid that Elena might change her mind, might refuse what he desired more than anything else on earth: the accomplishment of his plans.

Hanging eagerly and anxiously on her reply, the professor murmured: "When, Elena? When?"

"When you desire, my husband. The fire of my life is burning very low."

"This is infamous!" cried Giuseppe del Giovine, in an outburst that shook him from head to foot, so intense was his emotion. "Elena, are you, too, insane? Do you realize what you are doing? Cannot you understand that Filippo is quite mad with his visions? Even if what he has dreamed could be possible, do you know that you have offered him your death? Elena, Elena, give me your life! Put yourself into my hands! I will cure you. I know that I can cure you," he begged wildly.

The beautiful young woman looked sadly and understandingly at the impassioned doctor. She shook her head slowly. Then her eyes turned again to her husband. Giuseppe del Giovine realized that his interference was futile; Elena's life, Elena's death, both lay in the hands of the man she loved. And (cruel irony!) it was her death that would mean most to the man she loved.

The professor called a servant and issued hasty instructions; his rivals were to be summoned at once, to see the successful outcome of his experiment. Then he turned to his wife, elation shining from his glowing countenance.

"Help me prepare!" he commanded.

An expression of awful agony passed over Elena's set face, but she motioned the agitated young doctor indifferently from her path, and began to set in position various instruments on the table adjacent to that under the crystal bell.

"What are you intending to do, Filippo?" demanded del Giovine, grasping the exalted dreamer authoritatively by one elbow.

Filippo shook off that restraining hand with impatience.

"Watch, and your patience will be rewarded," was the answer, as he smiled mysteriously.

"But Elena will not die today," said the physician, his hesitating lips forming the words reluctantly.

"She will die today," affirmed the professor, still smiling.

"*Dio mio*! He is absolutely mad!" Del Giovine would have fled for assistance, but the horror of the situation rooted his feet to the spot. Moreover, an imperative gesture from the proud Elena held him frozen there, his questioning eyes on hers.

"When the bell rings, Elena *mia*, I shall free your soul from its earthly shell, on which the hold is already so frail, and let it fly upward into the crystal bell," murmured Filippo, more tenderly than his wife had ever heard him speak to her before.

"I did not believe you could do it," Elena said, strangely. "I thought you really loved me! Have you no soul yourself, my husband, that you can so relentlessly sacrifice a woman who adores you, to add fuel to the fires of your ambition?"

"Elena! No more, I beg you. You surely will not withdraw what you offered freely, of your own will?"

He turned his face from hers, lest unexpected weakness of the flesh might undo his will.

The doctor knew that Elena had risked her all on a single toss of the dice. Womanlike, she believed that Filippo would throw aside the everlasting fame which he hoped would accrue to him, instead of accepting, as he was doing, the sacrifice of herself.

With face still averted, the professor motioned his wife to place herself upon the table under the crystal bell.

She gave one dreadful, tearing sob. "For me, life has long since lost its value," said she. "I think I may be happier dead!"

She mounted the table and stretched herself upon it.

Footsteps sounded outside the door. Came a knock. The paralyzed del Giovine saw the professor catch up a glittering knife. And then Elena turned her face upward, and gazed so earnestly at the determined and ruthless scientist that he hesitated, weakening. Del Giovine saw the beloved woman of his soul push her lips together for her husband's last kiss.

"Why spoil this last exalted moment?" murmured Filippo harshly.

He dared not risk refusing her whim, for delay would be fatal to his plans; were not his rivals waiting for the work of entrance, behind the closed laboratory door? Leaning over his wife, he hastily brushed his lips against hers. She flung up her arms at once and caught him to her with convulsive strength.

The young doctor heard her whisper, "Farewell, unhappy man!"

Del Giovine struggled to throw off the almost hypnotic spell that bound him.

Furious at the delay, and hearing another knock at the door, Filippo jerked himself away from that passionate embrace. The knife flashed—plunged downward. Then he stood back, an expression of stupefied amazement on his face as he gazed enchanted at the crystal bell.

"It is her soul! Look! That pale mist of azure cloud that rises from her wounded bosom so lightly! See it sway and drift! Oh, ethereal vapor, now you are entering your crystal tomb! I can almost distinguish her features, Giuseppe. Look, how they change, almost imperceptibly, but surely, as the current of air moves out at the top of the bell to accommodate the entrance of her wraith!

"Why does she look at me so? She is pitying me—me! How can that be, seeing I am to be envied? Have I not attained in this moment to the loftiest pinnacle of my success? My triumph is complete! No—no— I need the envy—the jealous envy—the admiration and astonishment of my fellow-workers, to complete the glory of my success!"

Del Giovine succeeded in throwing off the lethargy of horror that had bound him; a cry burst from the hitherto paralyzed vocal cords of the young doctor.

The door burst open. Into the room rushed the little group of men who were confreres and rivals in science with Professor Filippo Panebianco. Wordlessly the triumphant professor pointed to the crystal bell, all eyes following his guiding finger.

"**D**io!" he suddenly screamed, in agony and despair. "I forgot to close the upper valve! See—see—it is wide open! And there—there floats upon the air the last soft, wavering fringes of that wraith that was the spirit of my wife!"

He flung himself upon the lifeless form of the woman who had loved him too well, and beat at her with maddened fury.

"It is your fault, Elena! All your fault!"

Someone uttered a cry: "He has killed his poor wife!"

"Secure him, gentlemen! He has gone utterly mad!" warned the doctor, springing forward.

By sheer united strength they overcame the mad scientist, who fought against them furiously, uttering incoherent phrases as he struggled.

"Why did I stop to give her a silly kiss? Oh, if I had not stopped, I would have remembered to close the valve, and the wonder of my triumph would have remained to cover with the mantle of success what they are pleased so stupidly to call my crime.

"But alas! I was always a tender fool! Oh, if only I could have remained firm against her, when she desired that fatal kiss! I, who believed I would never experience the emotion of regret, shall suffer remorse for that weakness until I die!"

The Scarf of the Beloved

Weird Tales, February 1925

The night was dark and gloomy, but for him it was better so; the thick darkness, the approaching storm, all made detection less probable. Lowering clouds, scurrying across the sky, dimmed the sickly rays of the pale moon. The wind, soughing in the branches of the cypresses and among the ghostly tombstones, seemed to carry indignant and mournful whisperings from those graves that had escaped the desecration the others had experienced. Ever and anon, the faint, scared chirp of some homeward fluttering bird came softly to his ear.

The night was almost breathless with expectancy of the coming storm. The lurid flash of the lightning made the dense darkness almost palpable. The fitful warning of those vivid flashes urged haste upon him; he must complete his work before the storm broke in its concentrated fury.

His spade struck heavily against a leaden coffin. He stopped digging and whistled cautiously for his assistant. In a few minutes the coffin had been pried open, and the shroud pulled out, bringing rudely with it the cold clay that lay sleeping so heavily in death's long slumber. Presently the body fell with heavy thud upon the bed of the wagon that waited just without the cemetery gates. The second man covered it with sacking, climbed upon the wagon, and drove away. The first man began to fill in the rifled grave with earth.

His task completed, he paused for a moment as he contemplated the mound rising above that hollow mockery of a grave. A sudden premonition as of evil about to fall upon him oppressed his spirit. With uncontrollable impulse, he caught up his tools and fled from the spot.

The storm was approaching apace. The muttering of the thunder could be heard more distinctly as it grew slowly in volume and then died reluctantly and threateningly away among the surrounding hills. The moon looked down from among the scurrying clouds, her pale and baleful gleams lighting the solitary scene with ghostly light.

Among the treetops the vanguards of the tempest rustled and tossed the branches with a sound as of souls sighing in durance. The usual calm night-calls of insects were hushed before the approach of the storm; only the occasional guttural croak of a bullfrog disturbed the chill hush that had fallen upon nature. A bird's timid, half-affrighted twitter came from the bushes near at hand, and the man glanced casually in that direction before turning homeward.

As he glanced, he descried in the moon's fitful light a soft, fluttering thing on the ground at his feet. He leaned down and picked it up. It was a woman's silken shawl, such a thing as his sweetheart wound about her delicate shoulders when the evening breezes blew chill. Whence had it come?

Even as he asked himself, he knew: it had fallen from the body of that dead whom he had disturbed in its solemn sleep. An involuntary shudder gripped him. He would have thrown the thing away, but that its finding at daybreak would have led to the discovery of the violated grave, which might otherwise escape observation.

The wind blew chiller, and yet more chill. Autumn had set in with a will, and was sweeping down on the wings of the flying tempest. The boughs of the trees swept lower and lower; the rustling among them grew more audible, more pronounced. It was as if the spirits of the dead were revisiting the scene of their last resting place, crying out in horror and loathing upon the man who had ruthlessly broken in on the slumber of so many of their sad company.

Whispering and murmuring and muttering among the trees, and rushing around the tall tombstones that shone with weird whiteness from out the surrounding gloom, the wind flung itself upon the solitary figure of the man, who stood as if frozen to the spot, his gleaming eyes fixed with a stony stare on the frail, shimmering, cobwebby thing in his hands.

Paler than the dead who lay so still in their quiet rest in the churchyard; colder than the very touch of death itself; rigid as the body when the breath has gone forever; there he stood, the epitome of awful fear. With eyeballs starting from their sockets, open mouth, dilated nostrils, he seemed the very personification of incredulous horror.

The landscape swept and swirled around him. The wind sang in his ears as water sings in the ears of a drowning man. It tugged and pulled and beat at him as he stood immovable, clutched fast in the grasp of an awful fear, a horrible surmise.

In those outstretched hands lay the silken trifle, upon which his gaze was fixed with terrible intensity. The scarf was that of his promised wife. Only too well he knew it—that shimmering, lacy scarf he had so often seen about her shoulders. It was hers—hers—hers!

It seemed centuries that he stood there, eons of agony through which he passed in a fleeting moment. The appalling uncertainty of the thing rushed over him overwhelmingly. The scarf was hers. How, then, came it about the body of the dead? Her father had never been a strong man; perhaps an attack of heart trouble—something sudden—. The bare idea that he had profaned that grave, the grave of her father, lacerated his heart with remorse.

He dared not admit to himself, in that moment of horrible dread and uncertainty, the doubts that began to assail him. His one idea was that he must see, and that immediately, the dead whom his promised wife had covered with the scarf which he now held nervelessly in cold, stiff fingers. Yet the unwelcome belief grew ever stronger that it was indeed the body of her father, which his sacrilegious hand had desecrated unknowingly. The body of that sacred dead must at all costs be rescued from the medical students; must be returned to its resting place.

Instinctively, while his mind had not yet consciously formulated the desire, the man's limbs bore him rapidly in the wake of the wagon, which had long since disappeared in the gloom. He walked rapidly ahead, hushing the thoughts that hammered and clamored at the portal of his brains for admittance.

The road was rough, and the way long, but he walked steadily forward, as if in a trance. That the storm had already begun to batter on the trees bordering the road, he did not even notice. The rain had not yet come, but the wind had sent reinforcements to aid the vanguard which, during the earlier part of the night, had been rustling and pushing about among the trees. There was a continuous dull roar, as the thunder grew in volume and came nearer. The noise of the wagon wheels had died away, but the dark figure in the road toiled painfully onward.

Now the lights from the medical annex, dim through the gloom and the mists of blurring boughs that swept backward and forward before the night wanderer, revealed themselves. The wagon stood without. He ran to it, panting. It was empty. He hurried to the dissecting room and pushed against the door.

No one answered his low call. He pressed his face against the window in a vain attempt to see within, but the curtain had been closely drawn. At last, replying to his impatient knocks, a hand lifted it ever so slightly and a face looked into his, blanching as it looked. For a moment the man outside forgot his errand in the chilling shudder that swept through him at sight of that face gloomed over with shrinking abhorrence.

There was a murmur of lowered voices. The door opened cautiously and two or three students whom he knew emerged and closed it behind them. Portrayed on every countenance was that same look of horror and repugnance and loathing that had so startled him in the face of that man who had looked at him from the window.

He pushed his way toward the door; they shrank before him as he advanced. He demanded entrance in a voice that he scarcely knew as his own, a voice that died away, failing him at the looks of dread and frozen horror on the faces confronting him. No one spoke. Each gazed at the others, avoiding his proximity as they might have avoided contact with a man stricken with pestilence. He thought he heard a whispered word—"Nemesis!"—but it came from as remote a distance as might have come a dream voice.

Once more he made his request, but now it was in the manner of one who demands. A student pointed wordlessly, and he gathered from the gesture that the way was open to him. As he grasped the knob, the students with one accord melted away from that spot, unhallowed by its associations with robbery of the grave.

The man crossed the threshold and the wind pushed shut the door behind him with its invisible, malignant fingers. He moved across the room, still holding the silken scarf in his nerveless fingers. He paused before the table, whereon lay the dead whom he had that night dragged out of the peaceful grave.

With a quick gesture he tore away the sheet that concealed the cold and lifeless clay.

A tress of hair, rich, waving, auburn, trailed upon the floor.

One horrible, dissonant scream of bitter anguish shrilled from his lips, reverberated through the room, and wailed out on the chill night wind into the ears of the shuddering students dashing across the campus.

The body was that of his promised bride!

Wolf of the Steppes

Thrill Book, March 1, 1919

Letter from Doctor Thomas Connors to Amdi Rubdah, the Adept, Teheran, Persia

To my dear Master, greetings:

Not in vain have I learned from you somewhat of the mysteries enveloping the human soul in its earth life. In my performance for the first time of the ancient incantations you taught me under the Persian stars, I have gained a vivid knowledge of the occult powers resident in the flesh-caged spirit of man and realize with rejoicing the impotence of Evil in the everlasting conflict with Truth, especially when that Truth is armed with the knowledge that is power.

In this packet I inclose a number of letters sent me by my friend and colleague, Doctor Greeley. They will serve as an introduction to my narrative, which will follow, and they will bring you to the evening of the day I arrived at my friend's house.

Extract from Letter of Doctor Andrew Greeley to Doctor Thomas Connors

Since I penned the above memoranda regarding the solvent you inquired about, I have had an adventure, a very romantic adventure for an elderly married man! It really should have been a young bachelor like yourself, Tom, to have gone gallantly to the rescue. Myra has become so fond of our heroine that she insists that we should adopt the young lady. Of course this would be out of the question until we knew more about the girl.

Now I suppose I may as well satisfy your curiosity. About two weeks ago I was motoring out toward Riverside about dusk to look in on a convalescing patient. As I approached the grounds of a large, handsome residence which I had observed more than once when passing, I heard suddenly a long-drawn-out whining on a quavering and eerie note that was most unpleasant; it changed at last into an undulation that sent my blood cold. So unusual was the howl that involuntarily I slowed the car to listen, in case the animal should give voice again.

I would have stopped entirely, had not a white figure with frantically waving arms sprung out of the hedge and charged upon me, springing on the running board with an agility and an indifference to danger that startled me. It was a young and very good-looking girl. Such fear stared at me out of her wild eyes that when she clambered in beside me and commanded me to go on I did not hesitate, but obeyed her agonized cry.

"For God's sake don't stop!" she flung at me. "If you value your life, go on quickly!"

With that I heard the crashing of a heavy body through the shrubbery, and looked back with a thrill of apprehension to see a pair of flaming red eyes coming toward us at such a speed that I stood not on the order of my going. I shot out of there, the little flivver snorting like a mad thing, while that weird howl wailed out behind us. Why on earth I should have had such a horror of that great dog I don't know, unless the girl's terror had infected me, but I certainly felt as if the devil himself were swinging along after us. I turned toward home at the first side road, and am under the impression that the beast only dropped behind when we got into the village; I can assure you I didn't stop to look behind me after that last glance.

My wife was much astonished at her husband's return with a fainting heroine, and she had her hands full, the girl going into one attack of hysterics after another. All that we could get out of her during the next few days was that her name is Vera Andrevik; that she is an orphan; and that it will be useless for us to ask further explanations from her. She insists upon the last point with a firmness as strong as it is inexplicable, for naturally much depends upon it in her own interests.

Until she has become more normal we must content ourselves with the meager information she has condescended to give us. Her strange whims occupy us at present, giving much food for thought. In spite of the sultry nights now, she will not sleep until both windows in her room are locked and the Venetian blinds drawn and fastened. She makes a complete tour of the house nightly, personally superintending the securing of downstairs windows and doors. Lastly she locks herself into her room. Her mysterious precautions have furnished Myra and me the most lively curiosity.

If you happen to hear of a lovely lost Russian heiress, let me hear from you at once! On the other hand, if you are asked about the whereabouts of a fair but mentally unbalanced young lady, communicate with me also.

As ever,
Andrew

Letter from Doctor Greeley to Doctor Connors, Dated the Week After the Preceding Letter

Dear Tom:

Since writing you last our strange visitor has been acting in such an odd manner that I don't know but that you'd better come over when you get a chance and give me your opinion as to her sanity. My wife declares the girl as sane as I am, but you know Myra; everything is to her what she wants it to be.

Vera Andrevik has told us nothing more than I wrote you last. I ventured one evening to ask if she couldn't give us her mother's address; she turned absolutely white, looked at me with such a ghastly expression of horror that I was much startled; then she fell back limply in a faint. Myra, of course, scolded me for my masculine abruptness; she thinks I should leave the management of the matter to her entirely. We are agreed that it will not be wise to question the girl yet, as it will take time for her to regain her supposedly normal nervous condition. But you can judge from the foregoing if the subjects of home and mother are taboo or not.

I mentioned casually to Myra, in Vera's presence, a half-formed intention to make inquiries at the residence where the dog belonged. Vera flung herself at my feet in an agony of terror, hysterically begging me not to enter the grounds there. She declared that she could not explain, but that if I did not follow her counsel I would bring such peril upon us all as I could not imagine in my wildest flights of fancy. I promised not to go, but not entirely on account of Vera's pleas and representations; I have felt such a growing horror of that place that I can't bring myself to go down the road in front of it. For a gray-haired old doctor that's going some, isn't it? The red-eyed dog's howl has affected me most unpleasantly.

In the meantime, our visitor refused to go out of the house except in the flivver, and then she wraps herself around with thick veils, regardless of the sweltering heat of these close days. At night she continues to lock herself into her room. When I remonstrate with her she says: "Do you suppose I like to do it, Doctor Andrew? Yet it must be done." She refuses to enlighten me further; she says she doesn't care to be considered a harmless lunatic. I feel like telling her that she acts fairly crazy as it is to shut herself up on hot nights without outside air, but what's the use?

I am positive that she has been under a nervous strain that has for the time being unhinged her mind. Come out when you can, Tom, and observe the case. I shall be deeply interested to know what you think about it. But, for the love of mercy, don't come blundering into the house without letting me know first! The bell has been muffled because Vera nearly has convulsions every time it rings, such is her terror of God knows what. She would probably go into a cataleptic fit if she happened to see you come into the house unannounced.

Yours,
Andrew

From the Same to the Same

Dear Tom:

I gather, from the pronouncedly mystical tone of your last letter, that you've been dabbling again in the forbidden arts, seeking for the unfindable secrets of the soul. Let 'em alone, boy; they never brought good to any one, and it's dangerous business, most unsettling to the brain.

Instead of puzzling out magic spells, come down for a few days and help me work out a few chemical problems in my laboratory. It's been a long time since you've helped me with research work.

I've another reason for wanting you here, and that—as you may have surmised—is Vera. Tom, that child is suffering terribly. Unless she can relieve her mind I fear she will permanently lose her mental poise. She declares she is as sane as we are, but says she cannot tell us the story that would throw light on her queer actions, because, if she did, we would believe her insane. Then she just sobs and sobs, and it is all Myra can do to keep her from going into hysterics.

Today she almost went into a spasm in the automobile, and for almost nothing. She and Myra were in the back seat. A chap just wandered right into the path of the car, and when I stopped the old flivver with a jerk he looked at Vera and smiled in a triumphant manner that was highly unpleasant. He was an odd-looking fellow; wore a gray fur-trimmed overcoat and a gray fur cap, from under which his long, straight hair escaped in wild confusion. His heavy, black eyebrows met in a nearly horizontal line across his forehead, giving him a strangely fierce expression which his eyes did not contradict; I thought the latter looked almost garnet in color, an impression which Myra verified. The hand nearest us was hooked carelessly into his coat pocket by the thumb, and of the four fingers hanging outside the pocket the forefinger was so long that the abnormality was very pronounced; I have never seen such a strange hand before.

Vera began to whimper, clutching at Myra as if in abject, uncontrollable fear. "Go on, go on!" she cried wildly to me.

I had no good reason not to humor her, especially as the man finally stepped out of our way. He stood there, deliberately reading our license number aloud; Myra heard him after we had passed. Now why on earth should he do that? It was entirely his own fault that he had gotten in the way, and the old flivver never so much as touched him.

All the way home Vera moaned and carried on in the most pitiful manner, imploring us not to let "him" take her away from us. Her heartrending pleas to Mrs. Myra, as she calls my wife—for she never uses the word "mother"—were enough to draw tears to the eyes of a stone image. Myra assured her that no one should take her away against her own will, and she finally quieted down. But we had a bad night with her afterward, for at dusk some confounded dog came into our garden and took to howling, and it got on my nerves to such an extent that I actually imagined I recognized the howl of my friend of the red eyes, of whom I wrote you previously.

Vera went into a frenzy of terror at the sound of those howls, and insisted upon going the rounds of the doors and windows with my wife to assure herself that everything was securely fastened. Her fear is infectious; both Myra and I have impatiently assured each other numberless times that we do not feel in the least wrought up nervously, but the fact that we have had to affirm our mental calm is sufficient evidence that that confounded dog's howling and Vera's groundless fears have together broken in upon our sleep sufficiently to start us both well on the way to nervous trouble.

I am beginning to connect Vera's terror definitely with the fierce dog that chased my car that first night; just what the connection is I cannot figure out now, but the solution may present itself unexpectedly. What complicates matters is the effect upon Vera of that stranger who practically held up our car this morning; can he have something to do with the mystery also?

Yours,
Andrew

Postscript:

Just opened the above letter to add another more recent occurrence. The fellow I nearly ran over in town yesterday turns out to be Vera's guardian, a well-mannered Russian named Serge Vassilovitch. About an hour ago he was admitted to my study. His smile, which is a ready one, reveals a double row of white, pointed teeth between lips as full and red as a painted woman's. There clung about him a strangely suggestive odor, most disagreeable to my nostrils; it was damp, musty, stale—it reminded me of the smells of the animal cages at the zoological gardens. Probably the heavy gray fur on his coat carried the odor. All in all, in spite of his really charming manners, his personality was not one that attracted; instead, it repelled me strongly, and I felt instinctive distrust of him.

He told me that my license number had served as a clue to my address, and declared that he had recognized his ward under her heavy veils, although how he could have done so is more than I can understand, for I would not know my own wife under the thick layers of chiffon Vera had swathed about her pretty face.

Vassilovitch took me into his confidence with regard to Vera, although I could see he wasn't very happy about shaking the family skeleton's bones in public. Poor Vera! Her story is tragic. Her father went insane and shot himself; her mother threw herself from a window to certain death under an insane impulse; Vera herself has been possessed, since her mother's death, with hallucinations so strange, so bizarre that her lack of mental poise could not be doubted for a moment by any one to whom she had told her story.

"Why, she believes," said he, with grieved accents, "that her nearest and dearest are persecuting her. She declares that I am her worst enemy—I, her natural protector!"

He asked me if she had told us her story, and seemed oddly contented—if I have observed correctly—when I replied that we could extract nothing from her in explanation of her extremely odd behavior. He shook his head sadly. "If she were to tell you her so-called story," he explained, "you would realize that she is mentally unbalanced."

As I have mentioned, Vassilovitch was a pleasant-mannered fellow, but I felt so uneasy in his presence that it seemed to me as if I couldn't bear being shut up with him alone, and I made an excuse to open the door into the front hall. Silly and womanish, if you will, but you know that what we call intuition may often be well founded, and I feel that Serge Vassilovitch does not possess a good influence. I therefore dissipated it as much as possible.

After his explanation I felt it only right that he should see Vera and that the girl should have the opportunity to give us her side of the story, which was certainly due to my wife and me, after our having taken the girl in, a complete stranger, as we had. Her guardian agreed strongly with me on this point, and said very reasonably that he felt sure, after she had told her story, that we would be only too glad to turn her over to his care again.

I called Myra to bring Vera, but my wife replied that she did not know where the girl was and that she had apparently left the house when she saw her guardian enter it. Here was a fine to-do! And Vassilovitch seemed terribly upset. He spread those red lips of his tightly against his sharp white teeth in a kind of threatening snarl, and actually demanded of Myra if she would give her word of honor that she didn't know where the young lady was. He left finally, but not without stating definitely that he would return in a day or two. Myra thought his words and his manner distinctly threatening. The menace was worse because of its very indefinableness.

Myra insists vehemently that Vera is not out of her head. "I tell you, Andy," she declares, "that the girl has had such a terrible nervous shock that she is afraid no one will believe her if she tells her experience."

Vera, it appears, had been hidden in the garret, and since Myra did not know her exact whereabouts she felt that she could conscientiously tell Vassilovitch that she didn't know where the girl was. Funny idea of truth women have! Vera insists upon remaining in the garret, where she can jump out of a window and die instantly at will, as she expresses it. Draw your own conclusions as to whether or not she intends to return to her guardian.

I am sadly disturbed, Tom. I simply cannot make head or tail of the affair. Myra says Vera is as sane as she is herself, and Vera weeps hysterically when asked for an explanation, crying that she will kill herself rather than fall into the hands of Serge Vassilovitch.

If you can't come down, write me your opinion, Tom. Whether the girl is mentally deranged or no, her guardian claims that she is not of age and that he can therefore take her to his home by force, if he can find her. I am persuaded that she would rather die than return with him. I am sending this special delivery.

Hastily,
Andrew

Telegram from Doctor Connors to Doctor Greeley

Will be with you tonight without fail. Don't let Miss Andrevik out of your sight under any circumstances. Tom.

Resumption of Doctor Connors's Narrative

I studied the young girl carefully during dinner.

All she said or did rang true. I felt convinced that she was as well poised mentally as any of us, but 1 sensed an atmosphere of nerve strain about her and saw the spirit of keen suffering looking at me out of her beautiful, sad eyes. However, in a case of this kind one can never make true judgment without extended observation, and I was sure that something would be said or done before the evening was over that would give me the key to the situation. Moreover, I had come to a conclusion as to the source of the trouble which I know you have already surmised.

We adjourned to the library, a small, cozy room, after dinner. Doctor Greeley turned on the electric fan, for Miss Andrevik insisted that all windows on the lower floor especially should be closed and fastened at night, and the evening was very close and sultry. We chatted lightly about nothing in particular, until I felt that the time had arrived for me to bring up the real occasion for my visit. I turned to Vera, and was about to touch on the subject lying nearest the hearts of us all when I distinctly heard—underneath the library window giving on the front porch—a singular whining, snuffling noise, as of some big animal nosing around.

Vera stiffened in her chair. I reached out instinctively and took her hand in mine; I was sitting near her. It was as cold as ice, poor child. Silence reigned in the room, while we listened intently.

We heard the noise of taloned feet, half padding and half click-ing, across the boards of the porch flooring; the soft thud as the animal—whatever it was—sprang over the rail into the garden; and then a howl burst upon our startled ears that fairly lifted Vera from her chair. She pulled her hands from mine, rose to her feet as if im-pelled, and with a wail of terror threw herself upon the floor with her head in Mrs. Greeley's lap. As she hid her face she moaned: "It is he! It is he! Oh, don't let him take me away!"

Mrs. Greeley looked across at me half defiantly as she smoothed Vera's head with her motherly hands. The doctor looked at me with a wordless inquiry that demanded a reply. I gave it, know-ing that at the same time I was giving courage to the poor tor-mented girl, struggling with the terrible memories of her horrible experiences.

"Miss Andrevik is no more out of her head than I am," I said aloud. "I am going to whisper four words into her ear, and they are so magical," I affirmed lightly, "that she will find courage to tell me the things hidden in her heart and which she has dared to disclose because she believed she would be thought insane if she told them."

How quickly the poor girl raised her white face to search my eyes for the help I promised! I made her sit once more in her easy-chair, and then, leaning over her, I whispered the four words into her eager ears. You know, dear master, what those words were. For a moment she sat rigid like one entranced; then the revulsion of feel-ing that swept over her bowed her, sobbing, while Mrs. Greeley almost glared at me in her fear that I had hurt the girl whom she had grown to love like a daughter.

"Oh, how can I ever thank you?" cried Vera. "Yes, now I will have courage to tell you, for I know you will understand. If you could only realize how I have doubted even my own eyes these awful days. Doctor Connors!"

Another long, quavering howl broke upon our ears. Mrs. Greeley turned to me with an explanation. "It's a big dog," said she. "I saw him come into our garden just about dusk this evening. He is a big, gray, shaggy fellow. He has been haunting our garden of late at night, and he has a most disagreeable howl. I don't know to whom he belongs, but I certainly wish they would tie the brute up at night," she ended a trifle angrily.

I exchanged glances with Miss Andrevik, whose eyes were eloquent with meaning, and answered her in kind. Then I told my friends the four words I had whispered into her ear and that had worked such a magic change in her whole attitude, loosening her tongue and removing her fear to tell her story. Of course it was only natural that Doctor Greeley should give me a look of penetrating and disturbed amazement; he thought my mind had given way. His wife contented herself with a look of simple inquiry.

"I see that neither of you understand my words," I smiled tranquilly. "I can explain later on. Just now I want to learn the details of Miss Andrevik's story, so that I may decide upon my course of action. Depend upon it, there is more here than appears on the surface."

Again our conversation was punctuated by that mournful, ominous cry from without. Vera shuddered, but without her former hysterical symptoms; she knew that she had found a protector who was able to guard her; her thankful eyes told me that.

"You may not have heard a cry like that before, Andy," I observed to Doctor Greeley. "But I have hunted all over the world, and, whether you believe it or not, that is no dog's howl; that is the howl of a wolf that you hear tonight, and a wolf of a very savage kind, too, if I am not mistaken. Miss Andrevik's story will undoubtedly throw much light upon the matter, although it may not only sorely try her courage in the telling, but will tax your credulity tremendously. Before she begins, I want to assure her that I can and will believe every word of her recital."

Once more I sought her glance, and her eloquent eyes thanked me. Then I requested the doctor to go the rounds of the house with me once more to make doubly sure that doors and windows were well secured. I turned lights on full in every room, merely stating that this was imperative, for I did not feel there was time for full explanations; it was borne in upon me that before day broke we would all have seen strange things. But as you had taught me, dear teacher, I made use of the Light, in its artificial form, to nullify the forces of evil which I knew were abroad.

Vera's story, as nearly in her own words as I can remember it, runs as follows.

Vera's Narrative

My parents were Russian, and I was born in Russia. Coming under political suspicion because he had consorted with men not in his own class, my father was given to understand that he would be wise to leave the country. Converting into gold his large holdings, he took my mother and me and came to America. Serge Vassilovitch, one of the men with whom my father's association had brought him into disrepute, followed us in the course of three years. As they had both been students of the occult arts, in which my father had grown deeply interested, he was welcomed with open arms and given a home with us.

I was about ten years old. I spoke English fluently, having had an English governess, a good but stupid soul. I had never known anything but happiness in all my short life; always I had seen my mother laughing and my father good-humored. Therefore, I remember with what amazement I began to note my mother's face grow sad when she thought she was alone and with what dismay I discovered her more than once weeping. All this was after the arrival of Serge Vassilovitch.

My mother hid her trouble from my father, and it was not until long afterward that I learned the reason for her tears. Serge Vassilovitch loved my mother, and desired to take her away from my father, whom, however, she never ceased to love. He urged his guilty love upon her, only to be rebuffed repeatedly. Finally he swore that my mother should some day go to his arms whether she wanted to or not, and for some time he left her in peace. Then it was that my mother began to look sad and to weep in secret more than before, for my father fell so deeply under the spell of our evil genius that whatever Serge Vassilovitch proposed to him was as though foreordained. This condition of affairs went on for four years. I had grown to be tall and womanly and a companion to my dear mother, for I was seventeen years old when affairs reached a climax.

My father went so deeply into the study of the occult arts with Serge that it became his own and our undoing. Night after night they pored over unhallowed books of magic, and although I am sure Serge knew well what he was about, my poor father was more weak and curious than he was wicked. He fell so entirely under the evil spell of that incarnation of Satan that he finally arrived at a place where he could not break with him, and actually believed everything Serge told him, even to entertaining suspicions of my dear mother. He drew up a will, as we discovered afterward, naming Serge my guardian and leaving in those hands all that should have been ours in trust; this shows you how deeply he believed in that vile man.

One day Serge's mad passion broke bounds; his years of restraint made him madder than ever before. He caught my mother to him, kissing her and holding her to him until she lost her strength and fell from him in an agony of shame at her weakness! She turned on him at last, then, telling him that another day should not pass before her husband should know how his friend had abused his confidence. Serge laughed at her scornfully. She told him that he must leave her roof at once, and he apparently acceded to her request. But although she little realized it, her momentary generosity in covering up the matter in her anxiety not to trouble my father became her undoing.

The following morning a child's body, mangled dreadfully as though by the teeth of a savage dog, was found in our grounds. We kept no dog, therefore suspicion did not attach to our household. But my father was closeted with Serge for hours after that discovery, and afterward he shut himself into his library, admitting no one. In the afternoon he came into my mother's room, where we sat embroidering, and kissed us both with a tender gravity which I felt portended something unusual. He laid a sealed envelope in my mother's lap, requesting her not to open it until circumstances seemed to demand it. Strange request! While my mother still sat staring with puzzled face at the envelope, we heard a muffled shot. We ran down and pushed open the library door. Oh, my poor father! He had died, an innocent victim to that unmentionable devil whose evil influence had ruined all our lives. In his hand he still held the revolver with which he had hoped to purchase immunity for us from what he feared might be our fate.

After the agony of that experience was over my mother wanted to take me away, but our stem, implacable guardian refused to permit me to go, and my mother would not leave me, for she had already learned of Serge's further perfidy from my father's letter, and she dared not leave me with him.

My father's letter remained a sad secret with my mother during the year that we had together. During that year my poor mother was tortured in every conceivable manner imaginable by Serge Vassilovitch. Fearing both for me and for herself, she never left me alone for a moment, yet even in my presence that monster never desisted from inviting her to his arms with a cynicism that in itself was sufficiently revolting to a high-souled woman. It was toward the end of that first year of her widowhood that my mother learned the inner meaning of my father's letter—learned it from Serge's own lips.

My poor father had been the victim of a most vile plot, and had taken his own life in the belief that in so doing he was expiating his unconscious crime. Under Serge Vassilovitch's spell, he had been led to believe that, owing to the magic arts they had practiced together, the power of metamorphosis into the form of a wolf had been bestowed upon him by certain evil powers. Serge had himself killed the child, and had shown the mangled body to my father, declaring that in the form of a wolf my poor parent had destroyed and torn the innocent. Imagine the consternation and horror of a high-minded man who had unwisely permitted himself to dabble in magic arts that had brought him to such a pass. His remorse was terrible. He felt that, having unconsciously committed one such crime, he might in future commit others. He believed there was but one way out, and like a true and noble gentleman he took that way, not even giving his beloved wife an opportunity to dissuade him.

The awful story of his supposed crime formed the contents of his letter to my mother. Oh, if he had only come to her instead of taking that final step! My mother knew that he had laid by her side all that night. She taxed Serge, who laughed fiendishly, and admitted that he had lied to my father, thus forcing him to take his own life.

"Clearing the way very thoughtfully for his successor," said he sardonically.

Struck to the heart by the horror of the revelation, my mother attempted to flee with me, but Serge had given out that she was mentally unbalanced; we were stopped and forced to return. With scorn and loathing in her heart, she rebuffed his suit daily. But one afternoon, as I sat with my mother, embroidering, I felt his eyes upon me strangely. He was regarding me with such an expression that I suddenly feared him horribly, sprang up with a cry, and rushed to my mother's side. She caught me to her with a gasp of such anguish that it seems as if I could hear it now.

"Was not one victim enough for you?" she asked.

"Well," he returned with insolent indifference, "I was just wondering if, after all, I ought not to prefer the bud to the blossom."

There was a long pause. Then my mother said in a strange, hard voice: "You have won. Give me this one night in peace." And she still held me to her, while her labored breath shook her entire body.

Serge went slowly away with a backward smile, hatefully exposing his sharp white teeth with an air of knowing triumph.

My mother locked the door. She barred the window. Then she sat down, pulled me down beside her, and whispered the whole awful truth to me. I listened, my brain whirling, for it appeared to me that what they said must be true; and that my mother's mind had been injured by my father's tragic death.

Little by little, however, convinced by her deadly seriousness, by my father's letter, and by my own emotions of fear and horror when in the presence of my guardian, I began to credit her. I saw but one thing to do, and that was to attempt escape, even if we died in the attempt. My mother was firm in her intention to kill herself rather than fall into those evil hands, and, while she said nothing to me, I knew she would not leave me behind her. We whispered our plans to escape that very night. With youth's optimism I knew I could find something to do that would support my mother and myself. And in spite of her anxiety, my mother smiled her lovely smiles at me again for the first time in months.

When the house was sleeping soundly we crept out on the porch roof, and my mother slipped down a pillar to the ground, turning to hold out her arms to me. I was halfway down the roof when my mother's voice rang out in an agony of fear and horror.

"Vera, Vera, go back! Save yourself! The revolver! My God, it is the wolf of the steppes!"

As she cried out to me I saw a huge shape as of some great shaggy beast spring upon her from the darkness, bearing her to the ground. Something raised its head from where she lay, her cries silenced forever, and I roused myself from my apathy of deadly fear to scramble back into my window, away from the horror of those terrible fiery eyes, red and evil, that looked leering upon me from over my unfortunate mother's dead body. My senses were failing me, but I managed to get back into the room, and had hardly closed and fastened the shutter before I heard the thud of a heavy body upon the porch roof.

My mother's words echoed in my dizzy brain:

"Save yourself, Vera! The revolver—"

I looked about me hastily in the dim candlelight. On my mother's dressing table I saw a revolver, and I caught it up, crying out to the Thing that waited without: "If you try to break in here, I shall shoot you. I am armed."

The Thing sniffed around the window frame for a few moments, then sprang to the ground. I felt my senses leaving me, and I fell back on my mother's bed, unconscious.

With morning came voices, shrieks, feet running here and there, knockings on my door. I dared not open; I was terribly afraid of everything and everybody in that awful house. I heard my guardian's exclamations of horror at the discovery of my mother's mangled body, and it seemed to me as if I could not live through those moments of intense suffering. How I got through the day without losing my mind I do not know; I do remember that I lost myself in periods of unconsciousness several times.

Toward evening came the voice of my guardian at the door, stern and commanding. "Open at once, foolish girl!" he demanded.

I kept silence.

"If you do not open to me at once, Vera, I shall be obliged to break in the door."

"If you try to come in," I replied with desperate bravado, "I have a bullet ready for you."

He laughed with cold scorn. "Hunger will drive you out soon enough," he commented aloud. "But it will be better for you in the end to open now than later."

I felt that his words hid a mystery too terrible for explanation. But I remained firm. I was convinced that between Serge and the wolf of the steppes there was some evil connection.

After a while he seemed to have gone away, for I heard no sound. But at last came a sniffing around the cracks of the door and the scratching of sharp claws on the panels. He had sent the Thing that had killed my mother! Oh, how pitiless he was! I had heard of the wolf of the steppes, but had believed it only a superstition, yet my intuition told me that that which waited without was not a dog.

I cried out to it to go away, and finally it went, only to come to my window, whining and snarling there and scratching at the shutters.

"Go away!" I called again, cold fear clutching at my heart. "If anything tries to come in at this window I shall shoot on sight."

The howlings died away. Ominous silence ensued. I heard only the soft thud as the beast landed on the ground before the porch. You may well imagine what a night I passed, knowing that perhaps the Thing waited beneath my window. Just as morning broke I peered through a chink in the shutter and saw it for the first time. It was a great, gray, shaggy wolf; it bounded out of the bushes and stood, with slavering jaws, looking up at my window with its evil, red-rimmed eyes. It seemed to me that those eyes could penetrate the slats of the shutters and could see me watching from behind them. It raised its head and gave a long, dreadful howl.

Then, as I looked, I thought my eyes must be deceiving me, for it stood upright like a man. As the light grew stronger from the rising sun, the shaggy coat seemed to turn into civilized garments, and there, suddenly, where the wolf had stood, was my guardian, gazing up at my window with venomous ugliness upon his wicked face.

This time I did not lose my senses, for I realized with what I had to deal. All the old nursery tales told me of the wolf of the steppes when I was a little girl in Russia came to my mind again. I knew that the werewolf was discredited in America and that if I were to claim such a thing about my guardian I would not be believed, and might even be called insane, as my mother was. There was but one thing to be done; I must escape, even at the cost of my life.

That afternoon I saw Serge go on horseback down the road, and seized the favorable opportunity, only to be disillusioned. My governess, with pity in her eyes, turned me back, calling one of the servants to her aid. I realized that I was being guarded as would be a mad creature, so I went back, locking myself into my room. I was weak from want of food, but dared not open the door again, lest my guardian should return. Late afternoon brought him to my door again.

I had by then planned everything. I told him that if he would permit me to have ten minutes alone after the sun set I would unlock the door then. I heard him laugh quietly to himself, and I knew what his thoughts were; he did not know that I knew him for what he was; he thought I was prepared to receive an odious lover, and undoubtedly he was already thinking of how he would mangle my body with his metamorphosed talons and his sharp white teeth!

He told me that as an earnest of my good intentions I must surrender the revolver. This I had not expected, but I rose equal to the occasion.

"I dare not open the door to you now," I replied. "But I will throw it out of the window."

"Very well, Vera," assented my guardian. I heard his footsteps retiring down the hall, and knew he would go outside to retrieve the weapon, which I had no intention of giving up.

I took a silver-mounted hairbrush from my mother's dressing table, opened the window cautiously, and when I heard his steps on the graveled path below I threw the brush with all my force as far as I could into the bushes. He ran to get it. And then I unlocked my door, flew down the stairs, out of the front door, and down the path, thanking God that this time no one had appeared to stop me and putting my trust in Him that there would be someone outside who could save me from the horrible fate that might otherwise await me, unless I took the sad alternative of self-death.

Hardly was I out of sight of the house before I heard a long and dreadful howl of fury. I knew that the wolf of the steppes had found my door open and the room empty. Fear seemed to hold my feet to the ground. I clutched at my revolver, giving myself up as lost, when I heard Doctor Greeley's automobile coming down the road. You know the rest of the story.

Resumption of Doctor Connors's Narrative

The poor girl hardly dared meet her friends' eyes while telling the almost unbelievable tale, but upon finishing she turned imploringly to Mrs. Greeley, who half avoided her eyes and looked inquiringly at me. I replied to her questioning look with a glance of assurance, and turned to Vera.

"My dear Miss Andrevik, there is every reason for me to believe your story, since I have been a witness of just such a metamorphosis in Persia. Lycanthropy is on the wane, because the waste places of the world—forgathering places for spiritual forces of good and evil—are becoming peopled, and with added population such manifestations become more and more unusual. You may rest assured that I do not think you insane, and until I can explain the matter more fully to your friends they must take my word for it that you are unusually well-poised mentally, else you could never have come through such a terrible experience unscathed."

Vera's next thought was that, as she was a minor, her guardian would be able to claim her legally. To this I replied that there was but one thing to do, and that was to remove such a menace forever from the world. That I was determined to do this you can well understand; the only difficulty in the way was that if I shot the wolf the dead man would remain on our hands, according to the laws of lycanthropic metamorphosis, and I really did not like to think of hunting up Serge Vassilovitch and shooting him down in cold blood—murderer though he was—in bright daylight, in order to assure his transformation into a wolf, which alone would save me from a charge of manslaughter. The only way out of the dilemma was to kill the wolf and then rely upon a certain formula which you taught me to use under special conditions to transform into the wolf form permanently the slain Serge Vassilovitch. The authorities certainly might wonder at a wolf's being at large in the town, but they could not object to its being killed, especially if it had attacked any of us, as it would be certain to do if given sufficient opportunity. My object was to kill it before it could do any damage, either to any of us or to outsiders.

I instructed Doctor and Mrs. Greeley not to let Vera out of their sight, and to keep all their doors scrupulously secured, especially at night. I bade Vera retire and sleep sweetly, secure in the knowledge that one who understood her problem was watching over her safety. When Mrs. Greeley went upstairs with the girl my friend turned to me, and with severe gravity demanded an explanation of my "idiotic rigmarole." I gave it; dear master, I gave it very fully and completely. When the sun's rays brought us respite from our guard I was still explaining to my very skeptical friend. I promised him a sight of the metamorphosis, which he admitted would be a convincing proof of my "theories." He refused to believe that I could have seen just such a transformation with my own very good eyes.

For three days we kept closely to the house, and on the evening of the third day I saw the wolf of the steppes slipping behind a clump of bushes in the garden, and felt convinced that that night would see the last act played out. I had provided myself with the necessary articles, and awaited with impatience for the darkness to fold down upon us. I had cleared all movables out of the library, so that there would be plenty of free space. I stationed Doctor Greeley behind one of the French windows with a revolver, and I arranged a morris chair at the farther end of the room, behind which I crouched. The window was left unfastened, so that, at a light touch from without, it would swing inward.

We had planned that when the wolf entered, as it undoubtedly would, unless it were warier than I gave it credit for being, Doctor Greeley would immediately close the window behind it, turning on the light at the same time. If the creature turned and saw him, he was to shoot; otherwise, I would get a splendid opportunity from my ambush to finish the night terror of Russia. Each of us was also armed with a hunting knife, in case we came into close contact with the beast.

All happened as we had planned. We had hardly been in place fifteen minutes before we heard the padding and scraping of the taloned claws on the porch flooring, and a moment later a sniffing at the window, which, at the touch, swung slowly open. The moon had risen over the treetops, and her soft light poured into the room, rendering other light unnecessary. I saw the animal hesitate on the threshold for a moment; then it came into the room with a single bound, and sprang across to the inside door opening into the hall.

For an instant my heart stood still with apprehension. Had we forgotten to close that inner door in our anxiety to plan for the entrance of the wolf? No, the beast paused again before that closed door, and then began to pace back to the window. My friend closed it quickly, but in so doing stood against the moonlight in full view of the werewolf. I rose from behind my ambush and took quick aim, firing almost simultaneously with Doctor Greeley. Which of our shots took fatal effect I do not know to this day, since both were in vital spots. The great gray beast lifted itself into the air with a single convulsive movement, while a terrible howl of pain and fury burst from it. Doctor Greeley sprang to one side just in the nick of time, for the falling werewolf, with its dying effort, struck and snapped at the place where my friend had been standing, then rolled back upon the floor, twitching with a dying spasm.

I turned on the light, and my friend and I drew cautiously near to the dead animal. Then I turned triumphantly to him, I must confess, and wordlessly pointed to what lay on the library floor. Clad in his gray, fur-trimmed overcoat, now stained with red, Serge Vassilovitch lay with staring, furious garnet eyes, quite motionless.

Doctor Greeley looked as though he could not credit his own eyes, and then turned to me incredulously. "I could have sworn it was a wolf," said he slowly, horror-stricken.

I laughed. "In a short time you will see, with your own eyes, the transformation of this dead murderer into the werewolf form," I promised.

"Seeing's believing," he retorted.

The shots had brought both women down into the hall, and we heard their voices outside the door calling to us. I opened the door a trifle to say that all was well and the wolf dead. Then I added that they would do well to retire to an upstairs room for a while, and that they were not to come down under any circumstances. While Mrs. Greeley did not realize the gravity of this injunction, I saw that Vera Andrevik understood what I was about to do, for her eyes opened, startled, she drew Mrs. Greeley from the room, closed the door, and I heard their voices as they mounted the stairs to seek Vera's room, where I knew she would hold Mrs. Greeley until I had finished my incantation.

I closed door and windows. Then I carried out the instructions that you gave me, dear master, inclosing in one circle the dead murderer and in another double circle my friend and myself. I set the brazier in position, poured the prepared powder upon the glowing charcoal, and called thrice upon the Spirit of Evil. The first time such a deadly silence fell upon us that it struck cold to the palpitating heart; the second time a rushing wind came suddenly from nowhere and seemed to center itself upon the house, shaking it as with an earthquake shock; the third time—oh, dear master and teacher, it is well that you taught me to school my soul against the emotion of fear! When I felt the approach of the essence of wickedness materialized I feared for my friend, and made him kneel within the inner circle, bowing his head upon his clasped arms. Then I braced myself physically and lifted my head high to meet whatever was to come. It was more terrible than I had imagined!

From out the now dense darkness gathered unseen forces that I felt were pushing and pulling against the magic circle of protection. I knew that an instant's weakness on my part would give them entrance. I dared not rely upon my own strength entirely, and from the depths of my soul I sent out a cry to Adonai for courage and endurance. And it came—it came! But the Evil grew ever stronger and stronger, and I realized that I must use every ounce of my will to keep fear from my heart that the magic circle might not break, weakened by my weakness. I kept my eyes fixed upon the dead that lay within the farther circle.

The moon no longer shone in at the windows but there was a light that seemed to shine from where I stood and my friend knelt. Also the light from the brazier threw flickering tongues of brightness over the room now and then. When the moment came that I knew I could bear it no longer I called with a loud voice upon the Evil that lurked in the shade about us.

"In the name of Adonai, I have summoned you, powerful Spirit of Evil, because ye dare not refuse obedience to the supreme power. In the same Ineffable Name I call upon you thrice to break the spell that permits this dead that was a man to remain man after death. Beast he became of choice, and beast he must remain. In the name of Adonai, I admonish you, give him not the form of man again! In the name of Adonai, I command you, keep him ever in the form of that beast which he chose to assume! In the name of Adonai, aid him not again, alive or dead! And now, begone!"

As I called upon the name of the Mighty One I felt new life and courage and power flowing into my veins, and I knew that I was speaking with authority.

I looked upon the dead that lay nearby, and saw that the change had begun, so I touched my friend upon the shoulder. He lifted his head cautiously; his face was quite gray and drawn, for he had felt the spiritual influence of that Evil near us, and he had not been prepared, like myself, to resist and defeat it. His eyes fell upon the other circle, and in the soft light of the brazier I saw them dilate with incredulous astonishment.

Together we saw the metamorphosis of what had been Serge Vassilovitch into the wolf of the steppes, in which form that base spirit must remain imprisoned for the allotted space. My friend is convinced now that my "theories" are not groundless!

As the last of the transformation took place I felt a glad lightening of my spirits, and realized that the Evil about us, which I had called to undo its work, was about to depart. The rushing of a mighty wind again whirled about the house and departed whence it came, and, as it went, the moon's light broke forth from behind the clouds that had swathed it and burst out in full splendor, throwing into re-lief the body of the great gray wolf that lay within the farther circle. I stepped from the circle and turned on a light.

My friend met my smiling gaze with a look that impressed me with the awe he yet felt after our experience. "My dear Tom," he finally said, "I agree with Hamlet most sincerely and fully. There are stranger things than we know of. Let it go at that, old man."

We both laughed, for the ordeal was over, and with its passing came a revulsion of spirit that was welcome.

The body of the dead wolf was turned over to the authorities the following day. I suggested that possibly it had escaped from some traveling menagerie, and my explanation was accepted on the face of it.

Miss Andrevik has been formally adopted by my friends, the Greeleys, and her father's fortune finally turned over to her in the unexplainable absence of her guardian, Serge Vassilovitch. She has become as light-hearted as could be expected of a girl who had passed through such a gruesome and grueling experience. I may add that her extreme youth and the love she now finds we all have for her may have had something to do with helping her to regain her girlish happiness once so horribly threatened.

There is no more to relate at this moment, master, save that I hope someday to bring Vera with me to receive your blessing. As yet I have not spoken to her, but our eyes have said much that our lips do not yet feel licensed to speak.

Greetings, O Amdi Rubdah, from your pupil,
Thomas Connors

Fettered

Weird Tales, July-October, 1926

Chapter 1
Barred Windows

It had been a glorious day, and a glorious trip. Bessie Gillespie, dipping paddle into her side of the well-loaded canoe, sighed such a sigh of repletion and contentment that her twin brother chuckled softly behind her.

"Think you're going to like it, Bess?" he inquired, his gray eyes darting this way and that, as the canoe made upstream slowly.

"Oh, Ewan, it's wonderful!" she breathed, tossing back her bobbed brown head to inhale the sweet fragrance of the summer woods.

"You're dead right, it's wonderful," the young man agreed. "I ought to make some ripsnorting canvases in this kind of primeval atmosphere. Jove, Bessie, but the virgin forest is magnificent!"

The girl drew in her breath contentedly, but her paddle hesitated a moment over the sluggishly moving stream that flowed darkly past the sides of the canoe in the shadow of the trees, letting sparkling drops flash in the occasional beams of light from the setting sun, as it shone here and there through thickly interlaced branches.

"The woods are getting thicker, aren't they? Do you think we'll be able to find the cabin before dark?" she asked, a bit nervously, as her hazel eyes turned from one darkling shore to the other. "It would be rather—oh, do you know, I'd somehow hate to be out here in the open after dark," she admitted, laughing just a bit shamefacedly.

Ewan's indulgent smile patronized all weak women, as he pushed his paddle briskly into the black waters and sent the canoe spinning ahead under fresh impetus.

"Right you are, Bessie. I can't say I'd enjoy it myself, exactly. It would be different if we had come prepared for out-of-door camping. But they told us at Amity Dam that we would reach the cabin before nightfall."

"Ewan! Look!"

Bessie had turned her brown head sharply to the left, and now raised her paddle, pointing it at a dark building that stood half-hidden among the thick trees, although at nearer approach a wide clearing was visible between it and the stream.

"By Jove, Bessie, that must be Dr. Armitage's place, that the natives told us about!" Ewan held his paddle in the water until the canoe swerved shoreward, then with a dexterous movement sent it swiftly to the bank. "No matter how exclusive the man feels, he can't refuse to set us on our way. I'd like to know, at least, how much farther we've got to travel tonight before we reach our own place."

"It ought to be very near here," Bessie contributed, holding the canoe steady with her paddle against the gravelly bottom of the stream.

"We'll ask. Surely this strange recluse cannot refuse to give a civil answer to a civil question."

Ewan sprang out and helped his sister to the shore, drawing the canoe safely up on the strand. Together brother and sister walked toward the building that loomed gloomily out of the fast-thickening dusk.

It was a sizable affair, built of rustic hewn logs, yet with a certain pretension that marked it as the property of a more or less well-to-do man. There was a garage, also of rustic logs, behind the house, although the roadway must have been so primitive as to be hard on tires and body paint. What particularly interested the Gillespies, as they approached closely enough to see the building more distinctly, was the fact that every window, upstairs and down, was protected with iron grating, like a prison or madhouse. The effect on the spirits was somehow not an agreeable one; the inference he drew from those iron bars made even Ewan shudder, and Bessie's smooth brow contracted uneasily.

"Ewan! I'm afraid!" All at once she caught at her brother's khaki sleeve, her hazel eyes wide as she stared ahead. "I—I'm sure I saw somebody peering from behind that white curtain upstairs in the room to the right."

"Jove, Bess, don't be a goose! What if someone is looking at us? That doesn't mean anything, sis. They would, naturally, you know."

"Oh, it isn't just that. It's—it's something—. Ewan, let's go back to the canoe. We—we can find our own way, dear, without asking here. You know—down in the hamlet they said Dr. Armitage was—queer—and his wife—maybe not quite—right."

"Bessie, get hold of yourself. The dusk and the loneliness are taking toll of your nerves," said her brother brusquely. "I'm going to have a look at these odd Armitages. From what the villagers told us, they will be fairly near neighbors, and it's just as well to get on good terms with them in the beginning. Come along, little silly."

Ewan strode up the steps into the wide rustic veranda that seemed to run entirely around the lodge, approached the great oaken door, and with the huge knocker of weathered brass he tapped imperatively.

Silence. Bessie, close behind him, timid hand in his coat pocket, whispered timorously, "Ewan, I can feel eyes on us."

The artist tossed his rumpled brown head impatiently.

"Jove, Bessie, you're enough to give nerves to a phlegmatic cow! Out in this wilderness people don't open their doors readily to complete strangers. Why—"

He stopped abruptly, for at that moment footsteps sounded within the lodge, the scraping sound came as of heavy bars being moved inside the door, and a moment later the door itself swung slowly open.

Bessie shrank behind her brother, wide hazel eyes on that gradually widening aperture, and a terrified expectancy of she knew not what to emerge from the darkness. Into the doorway stepped a man; erect, robust, dark-haired and dark-eyed; clothed in more or less sophisticated tweeds that proclaimed their made-to-order origin. Right hand cupping a well-shaped Vandyke beard, this man glowered with heavy gaze upon brother and sister, without speaking.

Ewan felt suddenly foolish and small-boyish. He was furiously angry at himself for this susceptibility, as well as at this strange man who had power to impress him so deeply. He tried to be easy and confident in his speech, but spoke stumblingly.

"We are—ah—strangers—about here," he began.

The dark eyes burned upon him and then turned with no movement of the man's head to rest steadily on Bessie's palpably frightened face. A slight softening came into that dark, heavy scrutiny.

"It is plain that you are strangers, or you would not be intruding here," said the man clearly and distinctly. "Tell me your needs and be on your way," ungraciously. "This section is not safe after sundown," he added, in the manner of one who unwillingly gives an explanation.

Bessie shrank behind her brother and twitched at his coat. Ewan jerked away from her in irritation.

"There's no sense in being rude, Dr. Armitage," said he, then, getting hold of himself in his resentment at the other man's inhospitable attitude: "My sister and I are looking for a small log cabin which must be somewhere nearby. I thought you could direct us. It is getting night, and—"

There was a soft movement behind the man in the doorway, and the susuitus of a woman's garments caught Bessie's ear. Staring beyond him, she glimpsed the dimly outlined form of another human being in the dim interior of the room. A woman! But— A sudden shiver went over her as she strained to see more clearly. It seemed as if the face of that woman were shimmering with phosphorescence in the darkness; and the eyes were glowing redly as if lighted from within by some fearful evil force. Was it the last light of the sinking sun, reflected from the glowing sky, that caused this—illusion?

"Ewan! We don't want to trouble Dr. Armitage," gasped the girl, all at once trembling sickly with a fear of she knew not what. "Let us go on. A night in the open—"

The doctor's rich voice interrupted her. His burning dark eyes were on her pale, frightened face with a kind of lofty pity.

"You will not have to spend a night in the open," said he, rather more gently. "The cabin you are looking for is about a quarter of a mile farther upstream. On the other side of the brook, thank God!" he added strangely.

Ewan turned on his heel without further ado, drawing his sister after him.

"We could have found it without troubling our agreeable neighbor," he jerked out, angrily. "I'm sorry we landed, to meet such boorishness."

"How long do you intend to stay out here?" suddenly demanded the doctor, advancing beyond his threshold as he spoke.

Behind him came again that suggestive rustling, as of autumn dry leaves, stirred by some creeping thing.

"As long as I find good subjects for my brush," snapped Ewan.

The doctor had followed brother and sister as they went down the rough log steps. His left hand went to his heart rigidly, and with clenched right fist he smote the wooden railing such a blow that the impact must have bruised his hand, which he now turned, opened, bent his gaze upon as if half dazed by the pain.

"Ewan, let us hurry!" begged Bessie in a tremulous, low whisper. "I am terribly frightened. He—he must be out of his mind."

"Right you are, Bess," her brother agreed. "Evidently the Amity Dam people got the thing mixed up; it isn't the wife who's insane, but the husband. Fine neighbors they'll be," he added truculently, as he reached the canoe and held it for Bessie to enter.

There was the sound of voices; low, restrained, but coming clearly to the ears of the two voyagers as they pushed off from the shore. One was a woman's voice; light, lilting, but pulsing with an undertone of significance that came ominously to Bessie, who could not help listening.

"Let me go, Dale! I—I mean to speak to our new neighbors," pleaded the feminine voice wheedlingly. "It is not nice that you should give them such a poor opinion of you. After all, we'll be neighbors."

The doctor's voice, heavy also with dark meaning, pounded against the girl's ear-drums, setting her to shuddering involuntarily, so terribly did the hidden import of his words affect her.

"Go inside, Gretel. At once! You know why you must…Night has fallen; the sun set but just now. Inside, I tell you!"

The woman's voice, raised, resentful, yet shrilly sweet: "Yes—it is sunset—and they have gone—and I so wanted—"

"Yes, I think I understand, but I am here to take care of just that. Their cabin, Gretel, is on the other side of the stream," said the man's baritone heavily, "for which I render thanks to your Maker."

"The water—keeps running—so fast! It draws a line between us and them," wailed the woman's voice, plaintively.

"Thank God for that, Gretel, if you can. If not tonight, you may, tomorrow," said the doctor's voice fervently. "And now, come in, I tell you," sternly. "Come, Gretel; I insist."

A woman's sobs cut sharply on the still night air. There was a scuffing sound as of a struggle. There was an outcry, smothered suddenly: "No! No, Dale, no!" Then the heavy thud of the great oaken door. Silence. Silence that palpitated with the menace of the unknown.

"Ewan, there's something terribly strange about those two!" cried Bessie, pushing her paddle agitatedly into the water. "I think they're both crazy."

"Nonsense, sis! It's the man who's touched. As for the woman"—he hesitated—"she has my deepest sympathy. Poor thing, all alone up here in these woods, cut off from normal social intercourse with other human beings! Whatever she is, I'm sorry for her."

The canoe glided along in the dusk between shadowy shores that crowded dark and ominous on either hand.

"I don't know whether I am going to like this or not," shivered the girl, timorous eyes roving from one side to the other. "I feel as if any minute something would jump out upon us, Ewan. Oh, what's that, lying across the water?" and she screamed and flung herself down in the canoe.

"Low bridge!" called Ewan.

He had seen it more clearly, that great log that ray across this narrower part of the stream from shore to snore, forming a crude bridge. The canoe shot under it and Ewan slowed its progress to look about him.

"Hand me that electric torch, sis. Look! There is our cabin. We're nicely in time. In a few minutes we'll be cozily inside, Bess, so cheer up, girl."

A bit back from the shore, with a cleared space about it, stood a small log cabin that to Bessie Gillespie's eyes looked very inviting in the last palely lingering daylight. With thankful heart, as if she had reached a safe refuge from some vaguely threatening evil, she helped her brother carry their belongings from canoe to cabin.

But even after he had long been asleep, comforted by the hot meal she had prepared, Bessie lay sleepless, thinking against her will of the burning eyes of that strange physician; his inhospitable attitude; his unseen wife who had so longed, in vain, to meet her new neighbors.

As for Ewan, his smoldering resentment against the doctor followed him into his dreams, for he tossed and moaned as he slept. Once he cried aloud: "Poor little thing—I'll help you!" at which his sister shuddered in the night, burdened by premonitions that weighed heavily upon her usually blithe spirit.

Chapter 2
The Newspaper Clipping

It was well after 10 o'clock one morning about two weeks later when Ewan departed to complete a painting begun several days before. Bessie was occupying herself as usual, putting the cabin in order for the day. The impression of that first evening had faded somewhat from her mind; if she thought of it momentarily now, it was only to dismiss her unreasoning terror of that night as a thing born of darkness and the chill loneliness of unknown, apparently threatening surroundings.

When she heard a masculine step outside the window to which she was busily tacking mosquito netting, she did not lift her eyes, and was correspondingly startled when a voice not her brother's addressed her.

"*Bitte, Fräulein,*" murmured a coolly ironical baritone. "*Ein Wortalien.*"

"Oh!" cried out the girl, shrinking back from the window, her thoughts flashing involuntarily to the fact that she was entirely alone in the cabin and Ewan beyond hearing.

"Please!" said Dr. Armitage, urgently. "Don't be startled. I know you are thinking that your brother couldn't hear you if you were to call him—but you won't have to call, I assure yon."

Bessie looked at him, this mind-reader, out of plucky hazel eyes, but could not answer. The doctor smiled. At that frank, amused smile all fright left the girl at once, for his face immediately lost its forbidding severity and became so gentle, so appealing, so boyish, that courage flowed warmly back to her heart and brought an answering smile to her own lips.

"It's very unfortunate," argued the doctor as if to himself, and he stood a little distance from the window as if to reassure her; "it's very unfortunate that the other night you took my solicitude for sheer rudeness."

"Solicitude?" murmured Bessie, with ironical emphasis.

Resentful color flowed into her brown cheeks so that they glowed hotly.

"That is what I said, Miss—"

"Bessie Gillespie," she murmured unwillingly.

"From some remarks dropped the evening you called, I inferred that the amiable inhabitants of Amity Dam had told you my name and disgraceful reputation," drawled the doctor, his heavy dark eyebrows slightly lifted as if in lofty amusement.

"If you treated them the way you did my brother and myself, I don't wonder that their opinion of you isn't very good," Bessie said.

"I am quite aware, Miss Gillespie, that I did not appear to much advantage that night. Take into consideration, please, that I came out here with my—with Mrs. Armitage—in order to keep severely away from all other human beings." His voice was stern, his face grave. "And then all at once you two appeared, to tell me you would be close neighbors, and the—and it was sunset," he added abruptly.

Bessie's full lips compressed. She did not speak.

"I can see you are still angry with me, Miss Gillespie. I'm sorry. But that is as it may be." He moved one foot uneasily, tracing aimless figures on the sandy path. "I would be glad, nevertheless," said he steadily, without looking at her but watching the movements of his foot, "if you could think more kindly of your neighbor, Miss Gillespie. Believe me, my visit this morning is a reluctant one, but prompted by a motive entirely altruistic."

"All of which is undoubtedly very interesting, Dr. Armitage," the girl retorted coldly, "but I have much to do this morning, and my brother will be returning for his dinner, and—"

"And you have no time to waste on a rude, uncouth boor like Dale Armitage!" He laughed hardly. "My misfortune! From your standpoint you are entirely blameless, Miss Gillespie. Still—at the risk of seeming yet more rude and brutal, I must prosecute my errand here, for it is a high duty laid upon me not by my own conscience but by the dictates of a yet loftier duty toward not only you and your brother, but all mankind."

Bessie shrank within her window, and cast a fleeting glance toward the cabin door. Thank goodness, Ewan had closed it when he went out. If this strangely talking man made a single suspicious move, she would pull down the window and run to throw the fastening bar against the cabin door. And then she would hunt for Ewan's police whistle. Her heart beat quickly with agitation, and yet she could not exactly persuade herself that the doctor was not kindly in his intentions, for his piercing dark eyes were bent upon her under their heavy brows with an expression that was quite gentle. Indeed, she thought it almost pitying, which was surely odder yet.

"I came here this morning to talk with you, because you are a woman. A woman's intuitions are finer than a man's. You ought to feel that I am in earnest when I tell you what I have come to say. For it is within your power to persuade your brother to leave this accursed spot at once, never to return," he finished solemnly.

Bessie's breath came faster. She kept her eyes upon the doctor's face, and again its expression struck her as being pitying to a degree that weighed her down strangely, yet made her sense his sincerity with acute perception.

"I want to warn you that if you and your brother remain here, you are doing so at the risk of a peril to yourselves of so frightful a nature that it would be impossible for me to lay sufficient stress upon its horror. Miss Gillespie, this locality is not healthful for a handsome young man. Nor for a charming young woman." He bowed gravely.

Again Bessie sensed intuitively his honesty of intention, and could not take offense at the implied compliment.

"So far I have seen nothing to endanger either my brother's health or my own," she argued.

"It is not to he expected that you could, so soon," replied he. "If you knew what threatened you, it would already be too late," sadly. "Oh, my dear young lady, believe me that I am very much in earnest when I beg, implore you, to leave this place; if possible, today. You do not know, you could not even dream in your wildest flights of imagination, what danger lies in wait for you if you remain. Urge your brother to leave here this very afternoon. The trip downstream to Amity Dam would not take you as long as coming upstream; you would get there before dusk, and be among human beings—"

"Dr. Armitage," interrupted the girl. "Tell me something. Is Mrs. Armitage—insane? I—I thought she was, that night. She—looked so queer."

"So you saw her?" said he, slowly, appearing strangely moved at this direct inquiry. He flung back his head, beating the palms of his hands together in a hasty, unstudied gesture of desperation. Then he turned burning eyes upon the girl.

"Would—her insanity—distress you to the point of leaving here?" he evaded cautiously.

She shook her head slowly.

"No. But I'd like to know."

"My child, she is not insane. I wish to God it were that!"

Bessie's startled, incredulous expression made him add, hastily: "If that were all, it would be nothing. Comparatively nothing. And preferable, God knows, to what she is."

"Then she isn't insane?" persisted the girl.

"Far, far worse," replied the doctor cryptically, sadly.

"But if she isn't insane, why must you shield all your windows with iron bars?" she demanded.

"Ah, the reason for that you would not believe, even if I were to tell you," sighed he, heavily. "Miss Gillespie, Mrs. Armitage herself agreed to those bars at the windows."

"Then it is something from without that you fear!" cried the girl triumphantly. "Well, I am not afraid of anything while my brother is here to protect me. I know there are bears and sometimes wildcats in these woods. I don't go far from the cabin, and Ewan is usually within call," she lied steadily. "And I don't intend to take him away from his painting. He shall not be cheated out of this summer's work," defiantly.

"Then you will not heed my warning, you foolish girl?" exclaimed the doctor, with angry impatience kindling in his eyes.

"It is unnecessary to address me in that impertinent way, Dr. Armitage," the girl reminded him with proud resentment. "I am not a baby. I am twenty-four years old. I see no reason why you should not treat me with respect."

Her caller sighed heavily, impatiently. He took the Vandyke beard in his right hand with characteristic gesture and stood gazing upon her—sorrowfully, she told herself in astonishment.

"Very well, young lady. Since you refuse to save yourself by discreet flight, perhaps you will listen to another warning of a yet more personal and pointed nature, Miss Gillespie," with emphasis upon her name, mockingly.

"I would prefer you to leave me alone!" snapped the girl, losing patience. "I have no time to dilly-dally, Dr. Armitage."

"Listen!" came the doctor's rich voice. He strode to the window where she stood, too startled to retreat into the room. "Under no circumstances invite my—Mrs. Armitage—across your threshold! Do you understand? You are not to ask her into your home. Is that sufficiently clear?" He thrust his gloomy face at her, his black eyes snapping dangerously.

"It is clear that you are not only a brute, but idiotically jealous in the bargain," Bessie declared, struggling to maintain an outward composure she was far from feeling.

"Good God!" ejaculated the doctor tensely, raising his face to the noon-day sky as if in desperation. "No wonder hell's inferno can be established easily on earth, when human beings are so suspicious, so harsh in their judgments, so mistaken in their hasty opinions!"

He turned again to the girl.

"Very well, then, stay!" he grated. "But you remain in these woods at your peril. Not only of body, little fool, but of soul," he finished sternly.

His sincerity was obvious. Bessie began trembling. She took hold of the window ledge to steady herself. He must be sincere, to dare speak to her in such a way. ("Little fool!" he had said.)

"I believe you are trying to tell me something, but I can't quite understand," she murmured, moistening suddenly dry lips. "I wish—I wish you could trust me enough to be frank, Dr. Armitage."

Such a melting look altered the severe, almost grim visage of the doctor, that Bessie Gillespie felt the choking of powerful emotion in her throat as if in answer to the feeling she knew must be moving her visitor's heart.

"Child," said the doctor very softly, "if I could tell you, I would. But this is a thing that no average human being can credit and remain sane. Unless—unless there is a more than human courage in that soul, a more than ordinary poise, a serenity, strong faith in a higher power. If I could only believe that you might trust me," he said gently, appealingly, "it would be a most beautiful thought to take into my heart, to comfort me in my black hours. If you could only believe me sane, poised, braced to do a duty toward mankind that will take the utmost courage, the utmost strength, of which I am capable—God, how it would help me!"

His dark eyes held hers. She could see his mouth working as he strove to control himself. Sympathy, pity for something she sensed in him but could not put into coherent thought, swept over her. She slipped one brown hand under the unfastened mosquito netting to meet his. The man without leaned over in courtly fashion. At the touch of his reverent lips Bessie Gillespie thrilled; her eyelids drooped; her breath came quicker.

"I thank you from the bottom of my heart, Miss Gillespie, for your expression of confidence. If it is God's will, the truth will in time be made clear to you, but believe me when I say that I hope you will never have to hear it! That is the kindest thing I can wish you. God keep you safe, nut-brown maid!"

He turned away and walked with great strides that carried him rapidly to the roughly hewn log that formed communication with his side of the stream. Just there he stopped, leaned down, and picked up a newspaper which must have been dropped by Ewan the preceding evening, when he returned from a trip downstream to Amity Dam. This he opened with a quick, nervous movement and began scanning it avidly. All at once he crumpled it, flinging it from him with a gesture of horror. He stood as if frozen to the spot, staring at it for several terrible seconds. Then he went reluctantly over, picked it up once more, smoothed it out, and began to read again.

Bessie Gillespie was not by nature any more curious than others of her sex, but these incomprehensible actions almost made her doubt the wisdom of her expression of confidence in that strange and mysterious man. She drew away from the window, but not so far back that she could not watch his further actions.

Dr. Armitage tore out a comer of the paper, thrust it into the pocket of his tweed jacket, and went across the log bridge with steady stride. The girl's eyes followed him curiously. All at once she saw his clenched right hand strike the left palm; his dark head go back with a startled air. Her eyes went beyond him.

Ewan was walking slowly from the woods on the opposite shore, and beside him, her lithe figure swaying with alluring grace, moved the slight form of a woman dressed in a pale green sports suit banded in white. The color set off her marvelous blonde beauty delightfully. Such flaxen hair as shewed in escaping tendrils Bessie had not often seen, and she felt, rather than saw, that the eyes under the brim of the soft felt hat that this woman wore pulled down over her forehead would be the clear blue of an April sky.

It was this unexpected sight that had caused Dr. Armitage's furious gesture, and he now quickened his step to approach the strollers the sooner. Ewan's attention was diverted from his engrossing and fair companion by the hurrying footsteps, and he turned his head to see the doctor advancing rapidly in his direction. Mrs. Armitage lifted her face, smiling, to Ewan, and then turned to her husband with a bored, indifferent air, as he went directly up to her, pulled the newspaper clipping from his pocket, and thrust it under her very eyes with the air of a man who has reached the final limit of patience.

His furious air must have inflamed Ewan, who struck at that hand, so that the clipping fluttered to the ground. Bessie could hear the voices plainly as she listened, hidden in her window.

"A gentleman treats even his wife with some respect in the presence of strangers," Ewan was saying icily, in a tone that his sister recognized with apprehension as one presaging an impending outburst of passion on his part.

The doctor paid no attention to the young artist, but addressed himself entirely to Mrs. Armitage, with the air of one who could afford to slight lesser matters in the presence of those of more importance.

"Do you realize what you have done, you fiend?" he demanded, in a voice that was almost a shout. "After all your promises? Do you know what this entails upon me now?"

Mrs. Armitage shrugged delicate shoulders with an assumption of long-suffering patience. Her eyes were not on her husband when she finally deigned to address him, but on the artist.

"My dear Dale," she said clearly, "you are beside yourself. Please control your temper. There is a third person present."

The doctor almost choked. He swallowed convulsively, hot color dyeing his cheeks darker than ever. His burning eyes flashed hotly.

"How dared you disobey me?" he said at last, finding his voice thickly. "I told you not to leave the lodge. I forbade you to make the acquaintance of these innocent people!"

"Don't shout like that!" snapped the artist, thrusting himself between the doctor and Mrs. Armitage. "That's no way to address a woman. Control yourself!"

For a moment it seemed as if the doctor would strike him, for he lifted one clenched fist and it remained for a flashing instant level with his shoulder; then went down, open. The hand seized upon the wrist of Mrs. Armitage, whom her husband jerked with almost brutal abruptness toward the lodge road.

Ewan ground out something between his teeth. He started after them.

Mrs. Armitage turned her oval, charming face around cautiously. She looked into Ewan's enraged eyes for a moment, then shook her head with a quick little movement of negation. But her blue eyes were quite pitiful.

"Are you coming, Gretel?" growled the doctor, pulling her toward him. "Don't presume too much on my indulgence!"

She cast a languishing and martyred smile toward Ewan.

"Yes—I am coming. Dale—you hurt me," she complained.

"Not as much as you have hurt others," replied the doctor sharply.

Ewan remained as if rooted to the spot, his eyes fixed on the retreating forms until they disappeared down the bank among the trees. Then he went back across the stream, and flung himself into a chair in the cabin, face moody, mouth grim.

"You must be careful, Ewan," his sister warned. "Don't forget that Mrs. Armitage is—is queer," she hesitated. "She may even be dangerous at times."

"Dangerous!" snorted Ewan scornfully. "That little delicate thing! Don't be a goose, Bessie. She couldn't hurt a fly, poor child. And she's all alone, in the power of that jealous brute! It's abominable!"

"Well, what can we do about it, Ewan? He's her husband."

"Poor little thing, she apologized to me so prettily for the beastly way her great brute of a husband acted the other night. She felt so keenly his total lack of common decency toward us. She told me he is frightfully jealous of her. He brought her out here so that he could have her entirely to himself. He was just furious, that first night, at the idea of anyone living in this cabin, so near her; man or woman," disgustedly.

Bessie got out a chopping bowl and knife absently, her mind busy with the conflicting ideas she and Ewan now entertained for their two mysterious neighbors. Ewan rambled on, occupied with his sympathy for Gretel Armitage and his resentment at the doctor's obviously brutal attitude toward such a frail young creature.

Of one thing Bessie was convinced: the doctor was a sincere man carrying some secret burden that at times almost overwhelmed him. That it had to do with his wife, she understood. He had called Gretel a fiend. He would not so far have forgotten himself, had not the provocation been a serious one.

All at once: "Ewan," said Bessie sharply, "go across the bridge and bring me that scrap of paper Dr. Armitage tore from yesterday's newspaper, will you!"

Chapter 3
The Key to the Lodge

Ewan brought Bessie the clipping dropped by the doctor, but neither brother nor sister could make anything of it. It was a short notice of a funeral, to take place that afternoon, of a child of seven who had died of pernicious anemia. What connection could there be between this child of another name, and the Armitages? Yet the doctor had blamed his wife for something connected with that news item, had spoken of a duty imposed upon him because of it.

In a vain endeavor to account for his words, his anger, his seeming brutality, Bessie had turned that clipping upside down, around and around, but all her curiosity brought her was part of an advertisement for facial cream on the reverse of the notice, and a bit of political speech carried over from another page of the newspaper. It was a hopeless puzzle. She could not reconcile it with Dr. Armitage's pleading that she believe him a sane man burdened with something that would test the sanity of a less well-poised mentality. Yet in spite of herself, whenever she thought of his smile and the quivering of his mobile lips as he tried to thank her for her intuitive expression of trust, she could not but feel him well worthy of her confidence.

Ewan, with sketching block and colors, left the cabin about 1 o'clock. He wanted to catch the glinting afternoon sun on some birches he had found in a lovely group on the bank of the stream a little farther up.

"If that crazy fool comes blundering around again, Bessie, have the goodness to close the door against him. I left my police whistle on my dresser; blow it, and I'll be here on the double-quick. He's a big chap, but he'd better not bother my twin sister," threatened Ewan, grimly ominous.

"I don't think he will come again, Ewan," the girl opined, but she knew in her heart that her words were insincere.

As promptly as if he had been on the watch for her brother's departure, the robust form of Dr. Armitage came over the log bridge a few minutes later. The sight of him set Bessie to trembling, for in spite of an innate confidence in his sincerity, her remembrance of his almost brutal treatment of his wife troubled her and made her nervous. She wished he had not come back. And why should he come, she asked herself?

He walked briskly across the clearing, directly to the window where he had talked with her before.

"Miss Gillespie?" came his low, guarded voice. "Will you do me a great favor, please? I want to leave a key with you, in case of any emergency down at the lodge."

Bessie crossed the room and went to the door, opening it wide as if to reassure herself of her confidence in her intuitions. At this action, the doctor turned from the window. He did not approach her, yet his smile, bent on her with warm significance, bathed the girl in a glow of approbation that somehow made her feel strangely happy.

"You are not entirely disgusted with the brute that I seem to appear?" asked Dr. Armitage, almost sadly.

"I don't understand how you can act that way to Mrs. Armitage," the girl said abruptly. "What can she have done?"

"That is just what I cannot tell you, you see," responded the doctor, his face grave. "It was something for which she was not, in a finer sense, responsible, and on the other hand, she was entirely at fault. It was a terrible thing, Miss Gillespie; so terrible that for the moment, when I realized the extent of the horror, I was too overcome by my emotion to treat her as a man should always treat any woman," he deprecated.

Bessie cogitated for a moment.

"My brother brought me the newspaper clipping that you tore out of that journal," she said slowly.

"You read it, then? Ah, but you do not know what it meant to me! It meant that I can no longer trust my—Mrs. Armitage's—word. I—I was foolish, unwise enough, to trust her. The result is—God, out of Your infinite mercy, help me to undo what she has done!" he cried out passionately, clenched fists raised shaking to the sky.

"Still I do not understand," persisted the girl.

Her hazel eyes were on the doctor's convulsed face, pity in their tender depths. He drew a long, deep breath, let his hands drop at his sides, and looked almost hungrily into that gentle, compassionate countenance.

"I wonder if in your heart you have the slightest idea of what your sympathy means to me in the fight I am waging?" he asked simply. "Until now, there has not been a human being in whom I could even confide sufficiently to ask them to trust me," complained he, with a contraction of his heavy brows as if in mental pain.

He had come by slow steps to stand before her as she hesitated in the doorway. Now she put out her hands all at once, pity in her eyes, that rested on his face with gentle feminine solicitude.

"You asked if I would do you a favor," she reminded him, not at once withdrawing her hands, which he had taken in his with the incredulous air of a man who beholds the unfolding of a miracle.

He let her fingers slip from his reluctantly, dived into his pocket, and brought out a key which he extended with hesitation.

"It is the key to the only usable door at the lodge," he explained. "The other is screwed into its place."

"Then your wife has gone?" asked

"Mrs. Armitage is at the lodge," replied he unwillingly.

Bessie looked at the key, then up at him, puzzled.

"Why do you bring me the key, when Mrs. Armitage is there?" she asked, slightly troubled.

"Because," replied he steadily, "Mrs. Armitage is locked into the lodge, and the windows have been purposely barred to prevent her from emerging."

At the girl's persistent gaze, asking questions that she could not well put into words, he went on: "Mrs. Armitage herself has agreed to being locked in. But she is afraid that a fire or a severe storm might create a situation, where she—"

"Oh, I see," hurriedly interpolated the girl. "You will be away overnight, and she wishes someone to have the key, so that she can be—can be let out—in case of an emergency?"

"I shall be away until tomorrow night," the doctor told her. "I have a sad and terrible errand to do; a fearful but imperative duty to perform, God helping me. I hope to return for the key tomorrow evening, Miss Gillespie, and I shall be grateful if you will keep an eye on the lodge when you can."

"Of course," agreed the girl impulsively. "Ought I"—she hesitated—"ought I to run over and call on Mrs. Armitage, so that she won't be lonesome while you're away?"

He turned his dark eyes on her, something like horror gathering in them until they shone darkly like mysterious forest pools. His face froze into a tragic mask of terrible significance.

"Under no circumstances must you cross that threshold, or ask her to cross yours," he said strainedly, his voice stern.

Bessie's astonished face, turned to his in incredulous amazement at such a warning to one of his wife's sex, prompted him to more explicit speech. His expression grew lighter as his somber eyes rested on the girl's gentle, ingenuous countenance.

"You are ignorant of what she is. If ever she accepted your hospitality, you would rue it to your dying day. And after," he added, darkly; "and after."

Bessie smiled. (When she thought—afterward—that she had smiled, sick shudders raced each other up and down her spinal column.)

The doctor laid the key in her hand.

"One more thing, Miss Gillespie. Please do not, unless there should happen to be a fire at the lodge, give this key to your brother."

She looked at him thoughtfully, consideringly. A smile, half wistful, came over his face.

"I hope you are not thinking me jealous," he said. "I'm not. No matter what you may think, I'm not jealous of—Gretel Armitage. If—if she were not what she is—I would let her divorce me and seek her happiness elsewhere, but—as matters stand—it is better for her and for the world," he breathed mysteriously, "that she remain Mrs. Armitage," with an intonation of irony. "You will keep this key yourself? You promise?"

Bessie nodded affirmatively.

"I thank you. You cannot know how much your kindness means to me. In case of an emergency—give your brother the key," said the doctor, all at once becoming hard of voice and manner.

"Why should not I—?" began the girl, when he stopped her.

"Because I do not wish to have you exposed to an infection that is so utterly horrible that you could not understand it—or believe—even if I were to tell you of its danger," said he, sternly.

"Yet you would expose my brother!" charged the girl, hotly.

"Because he is a man, and because a man must always risk something where a woman is concerned. Also—but I cannot tell you now. How chained I am! How hopelessly fettered! Later, when I return, I may tell you something of this plague that heaven has seen fit to release upon the world, and that I—I, only I—am in a position to check. Bound by duty!"

He turned abruptly and went over the clearing again, across the log bridge, his bearing royal. Bessie Gillespie put one hand over her heart to check its beating. She found herself pressing to her warm brown cheek the key with which this strange man had entrusted her, and began to sob softly in terror at her own emotions and the consequences they might bring in their train.

There was something strangely sweet in his confidence, yet the surety weighed down Bessie's spirits that somehow she and this man were not to remain strangers: that their lives were subtly interlaced by the inscrutable decrees of fate.

Chapter 4
The Coming of Gretel

Ewan brought in a half-dozen extra armfuls of wood for the cook-stove, while Bessie was getting supper that night.

"It's going to storm hard," he told her, dumping an armful of split wood on the floor by the stove. "The wind is rising every minute, and the sky gets blacker and blacker. There ought to be a full moon tonight, but there's no hope of it with these clouds. Nice to be cozy in here!"

Bessie, feeling under more than ordinary tension, walked to the door and looked out, for the dozenth time. The burden of the charge laid upon her by the absent doctor wore heavily on her mind. She feared a storm. What if lightning struck the lodge? She would have to give Ewan the key, and he would release the blonde Gretel and bring her to the cabin. The doctor had expressly forbidden this, for some inscrutable reason of his own, which she felt, nevertheless, must be a good one, such was the confidence that mysterious man had aroused in her.

"You won't go out and leave me alone, Ewan?" she begged her brother nervously.

The artist looked at her curiously, as he straightened up from depositing another armful of wood on the floor.

"Not getting nerves, Bessie, are you? I never knew you to be as fussy as you've been since we got here. If you keep it up, I can't stand it; we'll have to go back," he growled, half in earnest, half in jest.

Bessie stood against the door-frame, staring out at the darkening sky. There had been a gorgeous sunset, presaging fair weather, yet fast upon it had been the rising pile, the fast-scudding black clouds, and now the ever-increasing murmur of the onrushing storm that swung and swayed the branches of the nearby trees until it seemed in the dusk that they were stretching out giant hands to seize any blundering intruders and wreak vengeance upon them. The girl shrank back inside the doorway as an especially severe gust of wind caught at her apron, whisking it away from khaki outing knickers with unrespectful fingers. It caught, too, at the door, slamming it back against the cabin wall.

"Jove, Bess! Dead right, it's going to be a heavy storm. No, sis, I shan't leave you. Nobody could tease me out into such a tempest."

Ewan flung down another armful of wood.

"We'd better close up windows and bar the door. Ewan, if—if lightning struck the lodge—would you—would you feel you had to help—them?"

Ewan secured the shaking door with the wooden bar against the increasing tempest.

"Why should I, when her husband's there?" he growled. "We've no call to butt in. Unless," and his sturdy young body stiffened involuntarily, "unless that poor girl were alone, and we knew it."

"You'd go, then?"

"Naturally, Bess."

"Suppose—suppose she is—alone?" faltered Bess, her fingers going into her apron pocket, where it seemed to her that the lodge key was actually burning.

"If I thought Gretel Armitage were alone," responded Ewan sharply, "I wouldn't wait for the lodge to be struck by lightning, sis. Fancy that poor girl, in that jail of a place, with this thunder crashing and the lightning flashing, and all hell breaking loose! Like—"

Bessie screamed loudly, shrilly. A crash of thunder shook the little cabin with its detonations, coming simultaneously with a long, vivid flash of yellow lightning that paled into nothingness the dim light of the oil-lamp on the table. It was as if Ewan had conjured up that terrible response to his imaginings.

Before she could recover from the shock, Bessie found herself looking into her brother's almost frantic eyes, his hands imprisoning her wrists tightly. His voice was shouting furiously into her terrified ears, above the roaring and crashing of the storm. Never before had she seen him in such a condition of passion as he exhibited at that moment. To complete her discomfiture, the skies seemed to open, and the pouring torrents that descended in white sheets beat upon the roof and battered at the walls of the little cabin, until it seemed that only such shouts could have been heard; as if a shout could be the only normal mode of communication in that bedlam of maddened nature.

"Bessie, that madman's been here again! Don't deny it! You've been talking with him! Is she—is Mrs. Armitage—alone down there? Has he gone away and left her all alone, in that hideous loneliness? Answer me!"

"Ewan! You're hurting me!" she cried back, trying to twist her aching wrists from his frenzied grasp. "Let go of my hands! If I talked with him, it was my own affair. Let me go!"

She writhed away from him, crying out again in affright as another terrific crash of thunder with its accompanying burst of blinding brilliancy thundered down the forest ways, shaking the cabin until it seemed that it would be moved from its foundations

"He told you he'd be away? Is she alone there? Oh, Bessie, don't be so stupid, for God's sake! Think of that poor thing, all alone in this frightful storm! It's inhuman!"

Bessie jerked her hands from Ewan's grasp at last. She twitched away from him. As she moved, he caught at her apron, and the thin strings loosened at his pull. The apron slipped away. From the pocket slid the key, falling upon the floor with a metallic jingle that Bessie's oversensitive ears heard even above the roaring of the tempest.

Ewan saw it fall. He sprang forward; had it in his fingers in a moment; turned it over and over. Then his eyes sought his sister's, accusing, scornful.

"This key doesn't belong here, Bessie. It's the key to the lodge, isn't it? So this is the reason why you don't want me to go out into the storm and leave you! A woman's heart! Can a man ever understand why a sister should be jealous of another woman?" Then he stopped and for a moment stood alert. "Listen to that wind!"

To Bessie it seemed a mad howl of malignant triumph that came down the forest ways as Ewan seized upon the lodge key. She sprang to his side.

"Ewan! He left it with me in case of an emergency," she began.

"Well, what d'you call this?" inquired Ewan as he tore down his oilcloth slicker and buckled a rain-hat over his dark hair. "Tea party?" sarcastically.

"You're not going out in this frightful storm?"

"Jove, Bessie, what's gotten into you? If you were normal you'd realize there's nothing else for me to do. Be human, my dear girl. There's another girl, all alone if I'm to believe what you've let me infer, in a great jail of a house, probably frightened into spasms by this storm," sternly, "and you try to persuade me to leave her there alone."

"Don't go, Ewan!"

Almost beside herself, Bessie stood in her brother's path and laid appealing hands on his shoulders.

"I'm afraid, Ewan! Why should you leave me here alone, when I'm so frightened, and go off to comfort a stranger? Ewan!"

Ewan shook off her hands disgustedly.

"Buck up, Bessie. If I'd dreamed that you'd be acting like this, I'd have come out here alone," he told her scornfully. "Better put on some coffee and get out some of your extra clothes, for we may be drenched when we get back," he finished prosaically.

The sister stood straight, regarding him from wide hazel eyes. She was remembering with painful distinctness Dr. Armitage's strange warning: "Do not let her cross your threshold!"

"You don't intend to bring her here?" she protested, weakly.

"How can I stay there, when her husband's away, Bessie, and he such a confounded jealous brute? Use your head, my dear. Here she'll be with another woman."

Ewan unbarred the door. When he lifted the latch, the storm twitched it out of his hand and the door swung back as if opened by unseen spirits of the night, abroad in terrible potency, and expecting him.

"Bar it behind me, Bessie. And don't open it until I get back."

Ewan was almost blown across the clearing. A vivid flash of lightning showed him on the log bridge, the electric torch in his hand dulled into insignificance under that brilliant blaze from the open heavens. Bessie pushed the door to with main strength, barred it, and then sank breathless into a chair, far more alarmed than she dared admit to herself.

Ewan had gone to bring Mrs. Armitage to the little cabin, and it was this very thing the doctor had warned her against. "Do not ask her into the cabin. Do not invite her across your threshold," he had said. In her heart Bessie was sure that Dale Armitage had some sound reason for this warning command; that much her intuition told her. And now Ewan had taken the key, and had gone to bring Gretel Armitage into this place where her husband had distinctly said she must under no circumstances be brought.

Trembling now and then, as an especially fierce gust of wind swept the clearing, making the little cabin shake ominously as if about to take leave of its foundations, the girl finally got up and put on coffee.

Then she looked over her scanty collection of sports clothes, selecting a pair of tweed knickers and a flannel shirt. Then she sat down again near the fire, actually appreciating it, even on that summer night, for the chill in the air was as sharp as it was untimely.

Such turmoil and unrest was within her as she had never experienced before. It was an expectancy of something strange, something unwelcome, that she felt coming to a head. She could not help connecting it with that glimpse she had had of Gretel Armitage on that night of arrival in the woods, from the depths of the dark room behind the doctor, when the setting sun had shone redly in Gretel's eyes, and her white face had glimmered with unhealthy pallor through the darkness. That it was the reflection of the sun Bessie had long since persuaded herself; any other thought would have been unwelcome, impossible. Yet the bare idea that Gretel Armitage was coming into the snug little cabin, Gretel with her gleaming eyes, her vivid red lips, troubled the girl excessively. She told herself in vain that it was the impression she had received from the doctor's warning; Gretel's strange, enigmatical smile recurred to her again and again; she told herself uneasily that she had no real reason to distrust Mrs. Armitage—unless it were the doctor's warning, and it would be unfair to be prejudiced to that extent.

The coffee sent up foaming bubbles of fragrance. Bessie rose and pushed it back on the stove.

Outside, the tempest still roared, but the thunder seemed to have spent its force; there were only distant rumbles now and then, and only occasional flashes of lightning. When the girl felt it must be about time for her brother to return, she pushed aside the rough burlap curtain that shielded the window giving on the clearing and the log bridge, and drew up a chair, to watch for the dancing light of his electric torch.

There came a terrific rumble, like the threatening mutter of a subdued but angry giant, and in the blazing light of the simultaneous flash Bessie saw a clumsy and misshapen creature staggering across the log bridge, leaning against the wind as it picked its way slowly. The girl was on her feet, one hand against her thumping heart, the other to the lips that writhed in vain endeavor to stifle the outcry that forced its way between them; her face went closer to the pane as she stared.

Another flash of lightning and a low rumble.

Oh, it was Ewan! And in his arms he was carrying—! It must be the doctor's wife whom he held so tenderly. Hot indignation flamed up in Bessie's simple heart. That woman—!

In another moment Ewan was pounding on the door.

"Bessie! Open! We're drenched! Open, Bessie!"

Bessie flew to the door and raised the bar. From without, Ewan impatiently pushed up the latch, and the door, urged by the wind, swung back, framing him with his shrinking companion in the doorway against the night's pitchy darkness. In that passing moment Bessie's soul apprehended such a crowding evil as sent her forward, palms outstretched, a cry choking into silence on her lips.

Gretel Armitage, seeing no ready welcome from that unwilling hostess, took one faltering step, and then sank slowly downward as if fainting.

Ewan, flashing a furious glance at his sister, sprang to Gretel's assistance. He caught the limp form in his arms, and with the doctor's wife against his breast he crossed the cabin threshold and bore his drooping, lovely burden to a chair, where he let her down carefully.

Bessie pushed the door to, but it seemed to her that all the hideous medley of that night's terrific tumult had in some subtle wise entered the cabin with Gretel Armitage, for the wind died down; the clouds scudding across the sky began to show glimpses of light from the hitherto hidden full moon; and the final clap of thunder that had announced, as it were, the arrival of the unbidden guest, seemed to have been the final effort of the storm as it retreated behind the mountain peaks above the valley.

"Got some dry clothes for her, Bessie?" the artist asked. He was leaning over Gretel, chafing her hands solicitously, his manner anxious and disturbed. "She'll need them, I'm sure."

"You are drenched, Ewan. She isn't," retorted his sister, whose keen eyes had noted that Ewan's oilskin had been wrapped about Gretel, leaving him unprotected against the storm's onslaughts.

"Oh, I can change later," Ewan said indifferently. "Coffee smells fine. We can all do with some coffee, I guess. She's a trump, but she was about half dead with terror, all alone in that weird old place, and this frightful storm shouting and beating at her windows," he added, yearningly, as he watched the trembling of her eyelids. "Poor girl! Be gentle with her, Bessie."

Bessie's mouth drew into a straighter line than ever it had before in her life. Privately, she thought that the doctor's wife was in no need of her gentle ministrations.

"If you'll get into your own room, I'll see to her," she snapped, putting out cups and saucers.

Ewan rambled on.

"Poor little thing! Until we got to the stream, she managed to struggle along with my help, but at the bridge she simply collapsed. She couldn't have made it across that narrow log, so I picked her up and carried her. And at that, she was so weak she fainted, as you saw."

The doctor's wife moaned.

"How the water runs! So black—so swift! It blocks my way!"

Sbe lifted her flaxen head heavily. Her blue eyes opened with sluggish languor.

"Oh, my kind knight and rescuer!"

Ewan, self-conscious color flinging signals of betrayal in his cheeks, let her hands drop.

"Feeling all right?" he asked tenderly. "I'll clear out, so my sister can get you into some dry togs."

He slipped out of sight into the small room adjoining.

Gretel watched his going from under half-lowered lids, white, blue-veined, languid. Then she lifted them alertly, almost hardly, to meet Bessie's suspicious and resentful hazel eyes. An amused, superior smile wreathed her vivid scarlet lips. She lowered the white lids then over her eyes, as if to conceal discreet amusement at her situation.

"If you want to take off your dress, Mrs. Armitage, and put on these knickers and this shirt," Bessie began, with that chill cordiality women know so well how to use in dissembling inward dislike, "I think you'll be more comfortable. The coffee is ready for you."

Gretel did not trouble to reply. She stood up and loosened the oilskin coat, throwing it to one side. Underneath, Bessie saw plainly, the other woman was perfectly dry. Gretel's clinging silken sheath of shimmering green certainly became her dazzling fairness, and she looked with a mocking little smile at the plain and simple garments her hostess had brought her.

"Thanks," said she briefly. "I really don't need a change. I'm perfectly dry, thanks to your brother's care of me. And your things would hardly be my style, Miss Gillespie," she murmured sweetly.

Without a word, Bessie picked up the rejected garments and put them back on their hooks behind a cretonne curtain at the back of the room.

Mrs. Armitage, indifferent to her hostess's presence, turned to the door of Ewan's room, something subtly triumphant emanating from her as she stood there, beautiful, alluring. "You may come out now, Ewan!" she called.

The artist opened the door and emerged from his retirement.

"But you haven't changed!" he cried out, as she moved sinuously toward him, her green silks shimmering about her lithe form.

"My dress wasn't at all wet, thank you. And it suits me better than Miss Gillespie's things," said the doctor's wife.

There was that sharp interchange of glances between the two women that betrayed to both simultaneously their harbored, mutual dislike.

Bessie poured off the coffee in silence.

"Oh, Ewan, I am so glad you brought me here! I should have died of fright in that great, dark, creepy house! How the thunder crashed! And that fearful lightning! It was terrible!"

Bessie received the impression that Gretel was quietly laughing within herself, and that the doctor's wife was not at all afraid of the storm.

"My husband will be very angry with me," Gretel murmured, then, appealing with her soft blue eyes to Ewan. "Dare I tell him how you carried me across the stream?" she half whispered.

"I had to carry her, she was so terrified and so weak," Ewan said to his sister, still proud of his exploit.

"Over that dark, swift-running water," murmured Gretel dreamily. "And then"—closing her eyes in voluptuous pleasure, her white palms upturned on her knees—"and then—!"

"And then," Ewan took up her words in vaunting manner, "I brought you to my door in my arms. And you fainted on the doorstep, and I brought you inside."

"Across the stream! And over your threshold! Ewan!" Gretel drawled, languidly. And then she laughed a high, shrill laugh, that she checked suddenly.

A violent spasm of shuddering seized upon Bessie.

"That was just what the doctor said must not occur," she said clearly. "You should not have come out tonight, Mrs. Armitage. I am sure he will be displeased. You were perfectly safe at home," added the girl resentfully.

Gretel turned her inscrutable face upon the girl.

"Some day," promised she, slowly, "you'll be glad that I came. Some day you'll let me kiss you," she said, with some terrible, dark menace in her light words. "Oh, you shan't push me off as you have done tonight, Miss Gillespie!"

"Bessie!" rebuked the artist, in a swift undertone. "I asked you to be kind to her!"

Mrs. Armitage spoke up quickly. "My husband has prejudiced your sister against me, Ewan, but that won't be for long. She will be among my closest friends, before much time passes," she prophesied, her blue eyes full upon Bessie with strangely vindictive light blazing in them, unseen by the artist.

The promise, that sounded kindly, fell upon Bessie's ears like the knell of hope. She shuddered.

"So my husband said unkind things to you behind my back, Miss Gillespie?"

Gretel's shoulders twitched with inward mirth. "How stupid men—some men, Ewan—can be!" she flung at the artist, with a bewitching smile. "Well, tonight we are free of Dale's lowering presence," she cried lightly. "Let us enjoy these precious moments of freedom! Let us forget that he always comes—when I do not want him," she finished, sullenly.

Ewan went to her side as if drawn irresistibly.

CHAPTER 5
"YOU SHALL ALL BE MINE!"

"**D**on't sit up, dear Miss Gillespie. I can see you're sleepy," murmured the smiling Gretel pointedly, noting that Bessie had stifled an involuntary yawn more than once. "I shall do very nicely with your brother for company, and you can shut yourself into his room where our talking won't bother you."

"Most sensible thing you can do, Bess," drawled the artist.

"That coffee was too strong," complained the doctor's wife, with a charming little pout. "I know I shan't sleep all night. No, Ewan, you must not drink more or you will stay awake, too, and you must have sleep, after carrying me so far, poor tired boy."

Bessie rose reluctantly, at her brother's impatient signal, for all that she was heavy-eyed with sleep. As she turned in the doorway, she heard Gretel's dulcet tones, and saw Gretel's hand on Ewan's.

"No, Ewan, you are all tired out, battling the storm and bringing me in your strong arms. You shall sleep, tired boy, with your head in Gretel's lap, and Gretel shall watch over you, so proudly. And perhaps you will dream," went on the insinuating voice in a penetrating whisper. "Dream—Ewan—beautiful, strange dreams!"

"I'll sit at your feet, lovely lady," came Ewan's slow, drowsy voice. "Bessie, throw me one of those extra blankets, like a good girl. And—Gretel—if you should touch my hair with your satin fingers now and then—ah, how I should sleep!"

Bessie complied uneasily with her brother's request, but she did not lie down on the cot in the inner room. She drew the door to, then sat on the edge of the cot and let her disturbed thoughts ramble unchecked. So Ewan and the doctor's wife were already friendly enough to call each other by first names...What would the doctor say, when he came and learned what had happened? Bessie felt, in a sense, responsible, yet knew that Dale Armitage would not, could not, blame her when he learned everything.

"Sleep, tired boy, sleep!" came the crooning voice from the next room, with smooth, hypnotic suggestion. "Sleep—sleep—sleep! Dear boy—tired boy—sleep—sleep!"

Bessie's straining ears could distinguish the heavy, unnatural breathing of the young artist as he sank into obedience to those whispered words.

A long silence, broken only by those repeated words, "Sleep—sleep," and then Mrs. Armitage's voice, raised a little, called in an undertone: "Miss Gillespie? Are you awake?"

Bessie held her breath while flashing surmises and suspicions raced across her mental vision. Some powerful inhibition, as of a warning, fell upon her and she held her peace, feeling that her guest in the next room was listening with bated breath for the calm, even breathing that would indicate that she slept. Again came the call.

"Ewan is sleeping, with his head on my knees. I am simply perishing for a drink of water, but I dislike to rouse him. Will you bring me a glass, please?"

"She does not want water," thought Bessie to herself. "She only wishes to discover if I am sleeping or awake. I shall not speak. Let her believe me asleep. Then I shall find out why she wishes to be alone, completely alone, with Ewan."

A deep, patient sigh from without apprized Bessie that Gretel was utilizing her final weapon; attempting to rouse her to a feeling of pity. She maintained her stoical silence. And then, such a quiet fell upon the little cabin as she had never before experienced. It was a stillness full of menace; a silence alive with intuitive warnings of such a nature that she could not puzzle out their hidden meanings, but sat on the edge of Ewan's cot, shaking with nervous chills and struggling almost in vain to control herself against the threat of that dread quiet, that to her soul was screaming significance.

The night had grown still, also. The storm had long since died away; not even a distant rumbling disturbed the serenity of the summer silence. To Bessie, sitting with straining ears and alert consciousness, it seemed that if only a cricket could have chirped or a bird called, that silence would have been less ominous. For the darkness was full of—things. They seemed actual entities, those hovering, groping, crawling things that were the vilely evil thoughts of someone. They crowded all about her. She huddled back against the wall, cheeks blanched, hazel eyes staring open in the opaque darkness, her breath controlled softly so as not to attract their attention unduly. God, how terrible must be someone's thoughts, to clog the very atmosphere with that potent, evil influence!

At last she could bear it no longer. Something drove her to her feet, with infinite precautions against disturbing the sleeper—or sleepers—in the adjoining room. She tiptoed across the rough board floor and drew the door toward her until the opening widened and she could look out into the other room. At what she saw, the outraged blood leaped into her brown cheeks. Her eyes flashed with mingled scorn and indignation.

Gretel Armitage had loosened her abundance of flaxen hair so that it hung like a misty cloud about the young artist, whose head lay on her knees. She was bending over him closely, her face against his—Bessie was sure—behind that voluptuous veil of pale, rippling fairness.

"Mrs. Armitage!" cried out the girl sharply.

Gretel lifted her head with a jerk, somehow awful in its automaton-like stiffness, until the long, pale locks whipped across Ewan's calm face like writhing serpents. She swept one hand upward and drew the back of it across her lips, that looked more brilliantly red than ever in the shaded light of the kerosene lamp. The gesture was for all the world like that of the thwarted small boy caught at his mother's jam-jars, as he wipes off on his sleeve the evidence of his guilt. But her eyes, as she raised them flashing upon the startled and shrinking girl in the doorway, were not the sheepish, ingenuous eyes of a small boy; they were the bitterly hard, shrewd eyes of one very old in the evil experiences of life. Moreover, they held within their flaming depths—reflected perhaps from the kerosene lamp upon the table—the same angry red which Bessie had seen that first night in the living room at the doctor's lodge, a warning and a menace.

Gretel's parted lips curled back against her flashing white teeth, that clamped together with a clicking sound as of anger, but did not speak. To Bessie there was something worse than speech in the other woman's contemptuous silence. There was something about the writhing crimson lips, the wrinkling aquiline nose, the redly flaring eyes, that was infinitely harder to bear unmoved than would have been any sarcastic or harsh words spoken in that moment of detection.

The tension of that silence was broken by the young man, who gave a long, quivering sigh in his sleep. The effect upon the two women was entirely different. Mrs. Armitage drooped over the sleeper with a deep sound in her throat, almost like a snarl, and cast her arms about and over the young man's unconscious head like a dog that covers a choice bone to keep it from some other canine rival. Bessie Gillespie threw her brown bobbed head back and drew in a long breath as if to reanimate the shattered remnants of her lingering courage. She walked across the floor to the huddled pair and took her brother by the shoulder, loosening and pushing back Gretel's reluctant hands.

At the rough but effective shaking she administered, Ewan sat up dreamily, eyes still befogged with sleep, and put one hand to his throat, which he began to stroke, a puzzled expression on his face. Then realization came to him, and the blood darkened his face and neck warmly. Shamefaced, he sprang to his feet.

"Jove! I'd no intention to be so rude! I must have fallen asleep. Mrs. Armitage, I beg ten thousand pardons," he exclaimed, "for it was insufferable of me. Bessie, how could you let me do such a thing?"

"It was not her fault, Mr. Gillespie," said the doctor's wife pointedly, her hands writhing in her lap like uneasy serpents disappointed of their prey. "You were tired, and I—I really wanted you to sleep, poor Ewan."

She spoke now like a hurt, rebuked child, half drowsily, but her flushed face and lively eyes belied her words. A new force seemed to emanate from her. It was as if she had drawn, in the silent watches of the night, upon some secret source of nourishment.

"I think I'd better go back to the lodge," she continued, after a moment, with a covert glance at Bessie's still, white face. "You— you will escort me, won't you, Ewan? I'm afraid to try crossing the bridge; that log is so narrow—"

Bessie spoke up plainly, her feminine feelings stirred by Mrs. Armitage's assumption of ownership in Ewan.

"I won't stay here alone, Ewan," said she firmly. "If you must walk back with Mrs. Armitage before daylight, I'll go along, too."

Ewan glanced at the window. The morning gray was beginning to turn the darkness into shapeless shadows.

"It's morning already," said he. "You shouldn't be afraid in daylight, Bessie. Lovely lady, will you have some coffee before we go?"

Mrs. Armitage shook her head slowly, her flaxen hair undulating like pale serpents agleam in the lamplight.

"Thank you, no, Ewan. I've had—" She broke off as if in confusion, her eyes turning under their pale lids from Ewan to Bessie.

Something tugged at Bessie's intuition sharply. It was as if she were trying to bring back an old memory that kept elusively just around the corner from her. She maintained her steady gaze, and had satisfaction in seeing the pale blue eyes with their ruby glints lower under her fixed, accusing eyes.

Gretel was replacing her hair in its usual coils.

"The pins hurt my head, and it's so heavy, I let it down," she deprecated, feeling Bessie's eyes upon her.

Bessie did not answer, but she brought a Navajo blanket for her guest to wrap about herself on the walk back to the lodge.

"You insist upon going?" asked Ewan in a displeased tone, as he saw his sister taking her heavy coat from its hook. "It isn't at all necessary, Bess," he added with emphasis.

"I told you I wouldn't stay here alone," retorted the girl, decidedly.

Mrs. Armitage flung her hostess a keen look from under those modestly lowered lashes, then, thrusting one hand through Ewan's crooked elbow, set off ahead with her escort, leaving Bessie to stumble along as best she might behind them.

Arrived at the lodge, Gretel unlocked the door and turned to the approaching girl.

"It appears that my husband oddly enough left the key with you, a complete stranger. Miss Gillespie. But he's always doing queer things. Do you wish to lock me in now? So that you can go away with the key to my freedom in your apron pocket?" She laughed low, bitterly.

"I don't want the key, Mrs. Armitage. I would not have taken it at all had not your husband represented that you chose to be locked in, and wished someone to have it in case of an emergency. You are looking at the whole situation in the wrong light. When he returns, I shall explain how it happened that you came across the stream, into our cabin," she finished, "for that was what he told me must not happen."

"Shall you tell my husband," she cried tauntingly, "how your dear brother carried me in his arms, against his heart? Over the stream? Into his home? How he slept all night with his head on my lap? I think not, Miss Gillespie."

The doctor's wife laughed with mocking intonation.

"Shall I make Ewan stay here with me? Or do you want him to go home with you? Which will look better in my husband's eyes?" she said. "Ewan will stay with me, if I ask him. Ewan?" caressingly.

Like a man half dazed, uncertain of himself, the young artist took a hesitating step in Gretel's direction. Bessie uttered a little choking cry. She wound her fingers into his cuff and held tightly.

"That wouldn't help you, my dear girl," Mrs. Armitage observed indulgently, her amused glance taking in the girl's action. "He would always come to me when I called him. Always. Nobody can stop him—now—for he is mine," she asserted, malicious laughter in her voice.

"Dr. Armitage could keep him from following you," asserted Bessie, courageously. "He can hold you in check, Mrs. Armitage."

Her rosy cheeks suddenly mist-pale, Mrs. Armitage darted from the doorway. She thrust her face close to the other girl's, her pale eyes glinting redly.

"What has he told you?" she whispered with fierce eagerness. "Oh, I shall punish him for betraying me to you, you brown thing! He makes everybody fear me, with his lies!"

She caught herself, walked back to the door, took out the key and inserted it on the inside.

"Well, it appears that you and Dale have found something to dislike in common," she slurred bitterly. "And that something is Dale's wife. Well, my dear, tell him what you please. I don't know, and I don't care, how you will account for the key's being in my hands.

But don't talk too much, little fool, or I shall take your brother away from you entirely. Do you understand?"

"Ewan! Come—please!" Bessie tugged at her brother's sleeve.

Like a man entranced, the young artist stood, his eyes fixed on the doctor's wife, whose evil beauty flamed in that gray dawn like a thing not of earth but some other mystic plane. Gretel smiled with exasperating amusement at Bessie's anxiety.

"You may have him for now, stupid brown girl. I'm through with him tonight. When I want him again, I'll call him." Her soft laugh was cruel. "And I'll pay up Dale for bringing me into these woods to die of loneliness," she added sharply.

"Ewan!" Bessie was urging her brother anxiously.

"You'd be lonesome tonight without your brother, wouldn't you, girl? Well, I'll call you too, you little plump thing. Yes, I make it a promise. I'll call you first, so you won't be lonely. Just see how kind I am!"

Bessie succeeded in drawing her brother along with her. He went down to the river-path, stumbling as if half dazed, unseeing where his feet went. Behind them, ringing out eerily through the gray morning mists, sounded the pealing of Mrs. Armitage's strange laughter, note on note.

"Both of you? All three of you! Ewan—Dale—and Bessie!" the doctor's wife was crying, between her bursts of ghastly merriment. "You shall all be mine!"

Chapter 6
Wounds in Ewan's Throat

The day dragged for Bessie, who dreaded the doctor's return and at the same time longed for the meeting to be over. The personality of the man had so impressed her that she felt he would be just in the matter of the key. But what his attitude might be toward her too-forward brother she dared not conjecture, especially after the specific warning that under no circumstances was Mrs. Armitage to be invited into the Gillespie cabin. As for Gretel, Bessie felt that the doctor's wife was fully competent to look after her own interests.

All day Ewan was moody and irritable. He was indolent, too, with an indolence unlike his aforetime lazy moods, which inhibited his painting only. Although the sun shone, and sky and woods were magnificent in their allure, he lay flat on his back in his room, staring at the ceiling. At meal-time he roused, but ate with a lack of appetite that troubled his sister, who was accustomed to cook for a good trencherman. She thought him extraordinarily pale. When she looked in at the door for the twentieth time, she saw him with one hand at his throat gingerly.

"Throat sore?"

He answered languidly that it just bothered him. "Some insect must have stung me, Bess. Perhaps you'd better put on iodine just as a precaution."

She brought the iodine bottle. As he took his hand away from his neck, Bessie exclaimed: "Why, Ewan, something certainly did bite you! There are two tiny white-rimmed punctures on your throat, and there's blood smeared—"

Ewan rolled wearily off the cot and went to the mirror, where he examined his throat attentively. "Looks funny, doesn't it? More like a snake bite than a spider-bite," he mused.

He washed off the streak of blood and Bessie touched the two angry-looking spots with iodine.

Bessie suggested then that he take fishing tackle down the brook a way, where they had observed trout on their trip on the first day.

"It's so beautiful out, Ewan, that it's a shame to stay indoors," she told him.

"Don't even feel up to fishing. Feel tired out. Jove, hope I'm not going to be sick, sis! Well, I'll go anyway."

His sister watched the canoe slip downstream, with a mixture of relief and apprehension. She did not want Ewan present when the doctor returned for the lodge key, but at the same time she dreaded his meeting Mrs. Armitage, for no reason except her distaste for that lady. Also, she intended to question the doctor more fully as to his wife's mental condition; if Gretel were not insane, but worse, Bessie intended that the doctor should clarify this remarkable statement, in justice to her confidence in him.

About 4 o'clock her watchful eyes saw the doctor's sturdy form coming into sight. He drew up his canoe and walked across to the cabin. Bessie went out to meet him. The troubled face she lifted to his searching eyes must have told him that any secret apprehensions he had entertained were not without foundation.

"You have the key?" he queried, dark eyes upon her kindly, and he extended one hand, palm upturned.

Those world-weary eyes of his had heavy black shadows about them; his mouth looked drawn as if he had recently endured a severe nervous strain.

Bessie's voice trembled. She dreaded to add the new trouble to those secret burdens he was already shouldering.

"Last night there was a frightful thunderstorm," she began.

"And Gretel has been out!" supplemented the doctor quickly.

Bessie nodded.

"Oh, God in heaven, how long must this infamous traffic in human souls be permitted?" cried the doctor passionately, throwing back his head and apostrophizing the clear afternoon sky.

"I'm so troubled about it!" Bessie cried out anxiously. "But I couldn't help it. Honestly, I couldn't."

"It was your brother who let her out?" stated rather than asked the doctor. His face had assumed a heavily weary expression, but it was not angry. "Of course, he carried her across the brook? And at the doorway she fainted, and he picked her up and took her across the threshold?"

"How can you know?" the girl exclaimed, aghast at this mysterious knowledge of the preceding night's occurrences.

"History always repeats itself," answered Dr. Armitage significantly.

"I don't understand," faltered the girl.

The doctor bent dark eyes on her with stem tenderness.

"I am sorry, little brown wren, that you have been drawn into this wretched business, but you would stay, when I warned you to go."

"Perhaps I can help you," said the girl eagerly, then dropped her hazel eyes as warm color ran up into her face and neck at the betrayal of her own interest.

"For that ingenuous blush I thank you, child," said the doctor, a slight tremble in his voice. "But I should have known better than to have drawn you into this business. I should have let Gretel run her own risks," bitterly.

He picked up Bessie's hands, pressing them so strongly that she almost cried out with the pain.

"You are reproaching yourself because of your friendly interest in me, are you not? Because I am a married man? Oh, brown girl with the kind eyes, if only you could be strong enough not to let your pity turn into anything warmer! You could help me, heaven only knows how much!" He dropped her hands then and with a shake of his whole body recovered his poise. "What I need to know just now is more for your sake and your brother's than for my own. Except," he corrected himself, "that my conscience is involved."

His hand caught her under the chin. Ho lilted her face upward, scrutinizing her closely. He withdrew his hand with a sigh of relief. "So far, all is well with you," said he thankfully. "And now, tell me everything that happened last night, my child. Everything. Do not omit the most trivial word or action of my—of Mrs. Armitage."

While Bessie told of Gretel's coming, Dr. Armitage listened in silence. He saw in sequence the pictures of Ewan carrying Gretel against his breast over the log bridge; of Gretel's fainting without the door and Ewan carrying her inside. Then Bessie told of how Gretel had called her in the night, and of how she had kept silence, knowing not why. And at that, he groaned aloud, but bade her continue. She told of finding Gretel's face against Ewan's, behind that veil of flaxen hair...

"God! God!" ejaculated the doctor, dark eyes blazing with combined pain and anger. "Is this vicious circle of corruption to go on forever? And then, Bessie—?"

"We took her home early, at daybreak," the girl concluded. "She told me that she intended to call Ewan, and that she would call me, too. And you." Bessie shivered, lifting a pale, scared face to his. "Can she? Can she? And what does she mean by it?"

Again the doctor jerked her chin up, exclaiming as he did so: "Impossible?" He scrutinized her white throat closely. "No. As yet you are safe. But your brother—!"

Bessie caught at his sleeve in fright. "What has happened to Ewan?" she managed to ask, choked.

"Tell me, brown girl, has he complained of feeling weak and languid since last night?" asked the doctor grimly. She nodded. "Have you seen, by any chance, whether his throat—"

"Something had bitten him. There were two white-rimmed little holes on his throat, and his neck was smeared with blood. I put iodine on the bites."

"Iodine!" ejaculated the physician, with a shout of wild laughter that made the girl shrink back in momentary alarm. "Iodine! Since when can iodine save a soul?" he demanded of nobody in particular, but followed his words with another terrible, sardonic laugh.

"Then it's something serious? Something poisonous?" she faltered.

"Serious? Good God, yes! Poisonous? Brown Bessie, the most venomous thing upon God's footstool has attacked your brother, and unless drastic measures are taken immediately, he will lose not only his body, but his soul's salvation," declared Dale Armitage gravely.

Great tears rose in the girl's eyes. "You can save him, can't you?" she whispered hopefully.

"Do you believe that I can?" he parried.

"Yes! Oh, yes, I do!"

"God bless you, child," said he fervently. "Only He knows how much your simple faith means to me. Yes, I believe I can save your brother, but only if he puts himself completely into my hands, and I doubt if he can be persuaded to do that," sadly, "for Gretel has succeeded in arousing his antagonism against me."

"I will make him," said Ewan's sister with emphasis.

"Then we will do what we can, Bessie."

"But what was it that bit him?"

The doctor laughed. It was not the wild laughter of a moment since; it was the hopeless laughter of one who laughs because otherwise he might weep. "If I were to tell you, you would not believe me," he said.

"You are wrong. I would believe anything you told me."

"I wonder," said he, slowly. "Well, let me see how much you are capable of believing from my lips." A cynical smile, but his dark eyes were yearning, and Bessie felt her whole being answer that call for understanding and trust.

"If I told you, for example, that yesterday I attended the funeral of a child, in order to locate its grave readily this morning, could open it without hindrance, could expose that poor little bloodless corpse—"

The girl's eyes were staring, wide upon his face, but she moistened her dry lips and said firmly: "I would believe that you had some good reason."

"Thank you, brown girl. And suppose I told you that I cut off the poor little head? That I drove a sharp stake through the little wasted body into the stilled heart? That I filled the dead baby's mouth with garlic?"

Uncontrollable shudders shook Bessie, but something in her heart bade her maintain her courage and her trust. She quavered, her voice trembling in spite of herself:

"You must have had a good reason."

"Again, I thank you," he murmured.

At the tremolo in his voice, Bessie knew that he was touched to the core by her expression of confidence.

"And then I left the grave as I had found it, and returned here, and—and found that yet worse than that awaited me!" he groaned, all at once losing his forced composure.

He dropped his face into his hands despairingly. Bessie was at his side, her gentle hand on his arm. He lifted his face to smile wanly at her.

"You may have thought me harsh and cruel when I warned you against ever having Mrs. Armitage here, in your cabin. How little you felt the actual weight of my words you have shown by the tale of last night's occurrence. Oh, had you realized the fearful consequences of your hospitality, you would have stood immobile in the doorway, and have refused to let even your brother enter, if he carried her with him. You would have bidden him leave her without, to perish in the storm!"

"I cannot believe that anything would make me as inhuman as that," cried the girl incredulously. "What could possibly change me so? You owe it to me to tell me, now that you have trusted me so far."

He regarded her pityingly.

"I shall tell you—but not until I must," he responded. "And it will not be because I owe you the reason, but because I have made it the business of my life to keep—Mrs. Armitage—from committing any more gruesome murders—"

"You dare call your wife a murderess!" interrupted Bessie, gasping and shrinking from him.

"She is not my wife," said the doctor gravely.

"Not—your—wife?"

"Legally, yes. So that I may in a measure control her actions. But only a moral monster would dare to make such a—such a—to make Gretel Armitage his wife in anything but name only," dryly.

Bessie's brown cheeks flushed scarlet.

"I know that it is all a strange mystery, child. It is because of what she is that I married her—and because of it that she will never be my mate. And this, unhappily, has turned her love for me into fury. Out of a desire to be revenged upon me, she takes pleasure in escaping my vigilance, and then—because of her hatred for me she does these frightful things! The poor child whose little body I dug up this morning, that I might set its soul free, was slain by Gretel Armitage, in spite of all my precautions! In spite of all her promises to me, given time and again!"

Bessie's hands flew to her mouth, smothering a cry of horror and incredulity.

"You don't believe me, of course?" said the doctor patiently.

"I am trying to. But I read the clipping about the child. It died of pernicious anemia."

He smiled, shrugging his shoulders expressively.

"All this is part of the matter that I cannot tell you because you would believe me quite mad," said he simply. "Yet Gretel is the direct cause of that child's death, and because of it I had to go to-day to do what I told you. Partly for the child's sake, partly because the burden of Gretel's—being what she is—rests upon me," he admitted with a heavy sigh of patient resignation. "And now, can you still trust me?"

Bessie stood, eyes downcast, mien thoughtful.

"I believe you are sincere," she said at last. "As to the rest, I cannot understand it, but I believe that you do understand it."

Chapter 7
Wild Roses Blossoming

"**B**rown girl, you are a marvel among women!" cried the doctor, a kind of wonder ringing in his voice. "Yet I must save you while I can. Will you leave this place tomorrow? Oh, you do not know what it costs me in resolution, to put distance between myself and the first human soul that has shown a measure of comprehension for me in my frightful situation! But I must be strong," he added.

Her emotion overcame Bessie.

"How can you ask me to go away," cried she pitifully, "when you ought to know that I would never have a moment's peace the rest of my life, thinking of you—working out some hideous, ghastly problem alone—and thinking that I might have helped you somehow?"

"Child, child, you are breaking my heart," said he gravely, taking her wrists in his dry, burning palms. "I dare not think that you, too—? I have never believed that I could so quickly learn to care, as I have in these few pregnant days! Do not tell me that you, too, care more for me than casually? Oh, brown Bessie, tell me it is only as a friend that you hold me in your heart! It cannot be that you, too, care? Tell me that I am nothing but a friend, child," he pleaded.

Bessie hung her head; she could not give him the answer he desired. She knew all at once that he had become more than a friend. She realized that out of her pity and her interest had sprung a deeper sentiment, that was to chain her life to his more surely than iron bands could have done. Yet he was tied to another woman whom he did not love; another woman who wore his name.

At her silence the doctor groaned as if in such terrible mental agony that he could no longer contain himself. The girl raised pitying eyes to those burning ones that plunged their gaze deeply into hers as if to cool themselves. The convulsed face frightened her. She spoke his name in a little voice, trembling as she tried to withdraw her hands, gripped so fiercely now in his fingers.

"No, Bessie, do not take away these gentle hands," he pleaded in a tone so poignant that she desisted. "Let me hold onto them, and onto sanity for a little, before I go back into the yawning darkness of horror that awaits me."

"What are you saying?" she whispered. "What darkness do you fear, Dale? You—so brave—and fearless?"

His ugly laugh shook her anew with shuddering, although she knew it was not meant to frighten her. As if in reassurance, his grasp on her hands became lighter; he pressed her fingers gently, then released them.

"Bessie, my little brown Bessie! Why did you have to love me, and so thrust yourself into the most horrible tangle of infernal machinations that the world has ever known?"

"Dale," said she stumblingly, "there never need be any tangle because of me."

"Good heavens, child!"

"Isn't that what you mean?"

"Bessie, your innocent and wholly natural assumption betrays only too clearly how little you dream of the horrors into which you may be plunged unless you go away at once and leave me—forever. God forgive me for not having been more brutal in my behavior; perhaps then you would not have pitied me, you would have kept me away. How I blame myself for having brought that key to you! Yet, I dared not leave—her—all alone, and how could I trust—a man?"

"Perhaps God knew best when He sent me here," murmured the girl, timidly. "Perhaps somehow I can help you, Dale. If only you would let me know what I can do."

"Take your brother away from here," responded the man quickly. "If he remains in this vicinity and refuses to put himself into my hands for treatment, he is in such ghastly danger that the human mind would refuse to credit it, for sheer horror."

At the seriousness of the doctor's face, the gravity of his intonation, cold shivers passed over Bessie's body.

"But I am not going, Dale. I—I could not go, leaving you to face your problems alone."

"How can I persuade you? Bessie, I cannot bear to have you, too, fall victim to that poisonous Thing which Gretel has become."

"I am not a silly man," retorted the girl, wrinkling her nose scornfully at masculine weakness.

"And do you think your sex will save you?" asked the doctor ironically.

"I would be strong where Ewan might be weak, Dale."

"But you see, Bessie, that Gretel now has the entree to the cabin. Ewan has carried her across your threshold and welcomed her within."

"I would refuse to admit her," sturdily.

"She needs no welcome from you now," continued the doctor sadly. "The fact that your brother was within would secure her entrance. He carried her across the stream and over the threshold. And on his throat"—the doctor closed and opened his eyes slowly as if in pain—"are the marks that make him her slave for all time, unless he leaves this place at once and goes where she cannot reach him. Until those wounds heal, he is in her power."

"Then she can really call him to her?"

"Yes, my dear. And in time he will die like that poor child. Of pernicious anemia," he finished, in light scorn of that newspaper diagnosis. "He will be drained of his life blood, Bessie. God, girl, don't you understand, yet?"

"Do you mean that Gretel is a—a vampire?"

"If you consider me quite mad, it may frighten you away," said the doctor, with a short laugh. "Bessie, Gretel is a vampire. Do you understand that? Gretel is a bloodsucking demon. I am the husband of a living fiend. I am chained to her for her life by my own innocent act—"

"That will do, Dale, please. You can't frighten me off by shouting at me," Bessie said tranquilly. "So that is the secret. I've read of such things, but I didn't think they really existed. How did she ever get such an illusion?"

"Illusion? Are you quite sure you've understood what I told you? It cannot be that you would take the matter so calmly if you really understood it."

"Can she be cured, Dale?"

"Nothing can be done for her until she dies, and then I must do for her what I did for that poor child-victim."

"Then how can you cure Ewan?"

"If he persists in remaining here, and she gets at him again, I cannot cure him. If he goes away before those wounds on his throat heal, he will be beyond her jurisdiction."

"But she had no wounds on her throat," objected Bessie.

"That is such a long story that I cannot go into it now," said the doctor wearily. "Her inclinations have been so evil that she herself does not care to be healed, you see. Bessie, can you manage to get your brother away from here?"

"Can harm come to him, if he remains, putting himself into your hands?" queried the girl.

"How your interest in me weakens my resolution!" cried the doctor. "You are trying to coax me into letting you stay. Instead of arguing with you, I should be urging you to leave here at once."

"You did not answer my question," said the girl's soft voice.

"If he puts himself into my hands, he will be comparatively safe," admitted the doctor reluctantly. "But he will have to be watched constantly, or, under Gretel's compelling psychic influence, he will remove the very safeguards that I shall have put about him."

"I shall watch over him myself. She shall not touch him again," promised the girl fervently. "Now you must tell me how I can help you, Dale."

He leaned over and kissed one of her hands reverently.

"Just believe in me, brown Bessie. And if it chances that I die before her, you will see to it that upon her death her body is cremated, as my will directs. On a funeral pyre of mountain ash. They will try to keep you from doing it. They will say you are mad. But for the sake of an unhappy soul that through my inadvertence would otherwise be burdened by that awful curse, you must do it."

"I promise," said she with white lips. At last her indomitable spirit sensed that possible defeat she had not cared to admit. "But you won't die first, Dale!" she begged piteously, like a child.

"No, I won't die first," he comforted her gently.

"Ewan is returning!"

The girl's sharp ears had caught the sound of the water rippling back from the prow of the canoe, and the dripping of the flashing drops from the paddle.

"He will be furious to find you here," she murmured nervously.

"Nevertheless, he must find me here, Bessie. He will want to tell me what a brute I am," commented the doctor dryly.

He turned to watch Ewan, and as he looked, his expression softened into a great and understanding pity.

The young artist drew the canoe to shore as if even that trifling effort was hard for him. He picked up the fishing tackle and basket that came up so easily that one realized it must be empty, and started up from the bank with the weary, dragging steps of an old man. At the door his eyes lifted heavily, and took in the doctor standing nearby with Bessie. A flash of resentment came into that heaviness. Ewan dropped the basket and fishing tackle and took a hasty, stumbling step forward.

"What are you doing here?" he demanded belligerently, but as he came toward the two he swayed weakly and fell.

The doctor sprang, caught the fainting form, and carried the artist into the cabin, where he laid Ewan on the cot. He stood over him, looking down with gathered brow. The girl had followed, her round face pale with apprehension.

"He's not—?"

"It's the lack of blood," explained the doctor, absently. "He's been about drained. She—she'd been fasting," he murmured significantly.

"This is horrible!" gasped the girl sickly, the truth coming home at last with force.

The doctor caught her arm as she swayed dizzily and led her to a chair.

"You see, you didn't really understand how terribly true all I told you was. Now you're beginning to realize it. Sit still, child, while I make an examination of your brother."

He returned to Ewan; straightened the fainting man's limbs into a more comfortable position; pulled up the eyelids and looked at the dull eyes; drew the lips apart, that he might examine the teeth with meticulous care; pulled taut the skin of the throat and stared white-faced at the two odd little openings on the neck.

"Bessie, your brother is in pretty bad shape. She—she must have been ravenous. If it were not already growing night, I would put him into the canoe and leave it to you to slip down the stream to the town. Any risks you might take alone in the woods would be as nothing in comparison to those you face by remaining here."

The girl leaned back weakly in her chair.

"He isn't going to die, is he?" she whispered anxiously.

"I think not. At least, not this time," replied the doctor pointedly. "But we must take care that there isn't another time, Bessie. And to that end," he added as if to himself, "I have an hour of daylight, and I saw wild roses in blossom about a mile down the stream, on my side."

He turned briskly to the door after those cryptic words.

"Close this window, my child. Keep it tightly closed."

"But the night is growing warm and heavy, Dale. The air in here is so close—"

"There are worse things than close air, brown Bessie," returned the doctor enigmatically. "Keep all the windows closed, and also the door. Until I return," he amended.

"What shall I do for Ewan?"

"Let him sleep. Nature has her own best means of recuperation. When he wakens, give him bacon, eggs, thick slices of well-buttered bread. Plenty of coffee with evaporated milk. Don't stint him. He'll be hungry, I promise you, after he's rested a while."

He walked across the clearing, Bessie watching him. Then he came striding back again.

"Don't be alarmed if I'm not back before dark, Bessie. Keep the doors and windows closed until I return. I'll have to stop in at the lodge, you see. I must attend to Gretel before I return."

Dejection was in his mien and accent.

"I understand, Dale. I'll be waiting."

In those few words, Bessie Gillespie outlined her trust and her patience and her future policy in life to the man who went away comforted because of her sturdy simplicity and wholesomeness.

Chapter 8
Ewan Submits

Waiting was not to be as easy for Bessie as she had fancied. Ewan stirred on his cot shortly after dark, and when she flew to his side he begged her peevishly to let a little air into the room; he felt as if he were suffocating, he declared.

"I can't do that, Ewan. I promised the doctor—"

He sat up on his cot weakly.

"Jove, but it's exasperating to feel down and out like this," he complained. "Can't understand what's come over me. Bessie, fix me something to eat; that's a good girl. I'm half starved. Why, that must be it. I'm faint for want of food. I hardly ate this noon."

"Do keep quiet, Ewan," begged his sister earnestly. "Lie down—please. I'll bring you something in a few minutes. The doctor—"

"What's all this about the doctor? Why can't I get up, Bess? Must be a touch of grippe," said the young man, his hand going to his throat in a familiar gesture.

"Ewan, you fainted, and Dr. Armitage had to bring you in here."

"You were talking with him when I came back," accused Ewan. He sat up and leaned limply against the wall. "Jove, if only I felt like myself, sis, I'd rate you well. The fellow's married, you know."

"You don't have to warn me off, Ewan," retorted his sister, but her tones lacked conviction. "I might point out to you that Gretel Armitage is married, too, and that her husband might not be over pleased if he knew that you—"

She broke off abruptly. Why should she tell Ewan that she had caught the doctor's wife bestowing upon him her loathsome caresses?

More, that Gretel had—? Oh, she dared not broach that subject!

He would not believe her. She would wait. Dale would know how to tell her brother.

"Poor Gretel!" Ewan was saying languidly. "The fellow took advantage of her innocent unworldliness, and when her father died, he married her and got hold of all her money."

Bessie was momentarily indignant, but she relaxed, letting him talk on. So that was what Gretel had been telling him.

"And then he began to betray his jealous disposition. He wouldn't let her have a friend. Even children were taboo. When she did make friends on the sly with a seven-year-old girl, he dragged her off into the woods. When the little thing died recently, he wouldn't even let her attend the funeral or send flowers. Jove, he's a jealous brute!"

Bessie, listening as she turned bacon and broke eggs into the sizzling fat, felt resentment sweeping over her. So this was Gretel's version of the child's death. Incredible as the doctor's story would have been had anyone but himself related it to her, Bessie, with a loving woman's contrariness, preferred to believe it, rather than to accept Gretel's. Yet she was forced unwillingly to admit to herself that Gretel's story was more reasonable.

Presently she invited her brother to come into the larger room and eat. The inviting aroma of steaming coffee floated alluringly to the artist's nostrils. He rose weakly from the cot and walked into the adjoining room, where he sank into a chair, looking with the appreciation of a hungry man at his sister's culinary efforts.

"Is your throat better?" she asked presently, unable to keep away from a topic she very well knew she should have avoided until the doctor was present to make it as reasonable as such an incredible affair could be made.

Ewan put one hand to his neck; stroked it gingerly.

"Some spider, I'll say," he observed. "It feels as if all of me had been drawn into my neck," he smiled, wincing.

Bessie could have shrieked her new knowledge at him. "And so it is," she felt like crying in terrible warning. "And so it is!"

"I suppose the doctor could give me something to put on it?" Ewan continued, half reluctantly.

"I'm glad you're not going to let any silly prejudice against him stand in your way when you need him," commented his sister gravely. "He saw those wounds on your neck, Ewan, and is much disturbed."

"Over a spider's bite?" asked Ewan mockingly. "Just like a doctor to exaggerate the thing, so that a cure will appear marvelous."

"A very venomous creature attacked you, Ewan," responded his sister, with such seriousness that Ewan's fork paused on its way to his mouth, and he stared hard at her.

"Jove! And this creature is—?"

"He'll explain everything when he comes," she evaded, for the subject she had so carelessly introduced had gone a little beyond what she had intended.

"I see," said Ewan shortly. "And I presume he'll also explain why he visits my sister so frequently behind my back?"

"It will be intolerable if you start anything of that kind!" cried the girl passionately. "Haven't I a right to consult a physician if I choose?"

"Ah!" Ewan stared at her again. "Well, it all depends upon what attitude he takes with regard to that poor little lonely wife of his. More bacon and another egg, please, sis."

Bessie refilled his plate in silence. She was relieved when she saw the dancing light of a flashlight coming across the log bridge.

"Ewan, he's coming. Please be nice to him," she begged.

Her brother regarded her with drawn brow.

"Bessie, this is the first time I've known you to be really interested in a man. And he has to be married," he grunted, half in disgust.

"It's the first time I've known you to take up the cudgels in defense of a married woman," she put in quickly.

"Oh, for the Lord's sake, Bessie!"

"Well, be decent, then," said the girl in a tense undertone, as the doctor's flashlight approached the doorway and hesitated without, dancing on the window and through it upon the cabin roof.

"Let him in, will you?" Ewan said shortly, as Bessie hesitated. "He comes as a physician, doesn't he?"

She flew to the door and opened it.

The doctor came striding in, pushing the door to behind him

and putting the bar into place with a caution that stirred the artist's curiosity and Bessie's apprehension.

"Feeling better after a good supper?" he asked Ewan pleasantly.

The artist took his cue from the other's finely impersonal tone.

"My neck's a bit sore," said he, touching it and wincing a bit.

The doctor nodded with contracted brows and a quick glance at Bessie.

"Anything you can do for it?" continued Ewan. "It—it seems to be—drawing me so," he added distastefully. "And if it was something venomous that hit me, as Bessie says you told her—"

"What bit you, Mr. Gillespie, was a creature so venomous that I hardly dare encourage you very much in feeling sanguine about consequences unless you agree to put yourself unreservedly into my hands for such treatment as I may outline, no matter how absurd or inadequate such treatment may appear to you just now," said the doctor gravely.

Ewan gave a short, dry laugh. "You don't mean that these tiny punctures on my neck may prove fatal?" he asked incredulously, and at the other's grave inclination of the head he laughed again. "Bessie, do you make any sense out of that? I've never heard that there was any insect in these woods that could give a fatal bite."

"Did I say 'insect'?" asked the doctor very quietly.

Ewan twisted about in his chair, the better to observe the doctor's face.

"Are you joking at my expense?" he inquired, with an assumption of offended dignity.

"No, Mr. Gillespie, I am not joking. I am in deadly earnest."

"Then please explain yourself," demanded the artist, pushing back his chair and looking imperatively at the other man.

The doctor hesitated. He sighed heavily, and then, without Ewan's invitation, drew up a chair to the opposite side of the table and seated himself with deliberation.

"If I were to tell you outright what has happened, you would refuse to believe my explanation," he said finally. "Can you not just trust my statement that your wounds—which appear so trifling—are of an importance that cannot be exaggerated? That unless they are healed within a few days you are in danger of losing your life, to say nothing of what is far more important to you than life—your immortal soul?"

"You are not talking to a baby, Dr. Armitage," retorted the artist nervously, feeling in his pocket for a cigarette case. "Do you object to a sick man's smoking? It may help to settle my nerves after your wonderfully clear statement," he finished ironically.

The doctor accepted a cigarette, and replied with obvious reluctance: "You are a baby, Mr. Gillespie, when it comes to matters medical. If I were to give you in technical terms the story of what has happened to your throat, and what is liable to happen to you unless drastic steps are taken at once, you will admit that you would most likely be unable to understand those technical terms?"

"I agree with you there." Ewan coolly puffed his cigarette. "But why should you hesitate to tell me in non-technical terms what bit me? And the effect of this bite upon the human system? Always in non-technical terms. And the proper measures to be taken to heal these dangerous wounds?" he finished sarcastically.

"I do not tell you, because you would consider me a madman," replied the doctor with conviction. "And, considering me out of my mind, you would hardly credit or carry out my means of protection from further infection, would you?"

"I suppose not," Ewan said after a short pause.

"I will make a bargain with you," offered the doctor thoughtfully. "If you will put yourself into my hands and let me provide such measures of precaution for the healing of that dangerous infection which is even now creeping over your system"—Ewan's hand went to his throat again; and his face was startled as he listened—"when you have been healed I will tell you all that I feel I cannot wisely tell you at this time, when your confidence in me is so absolutely necessary that I dare not risk losing an iota of any faith you may have in me as a medical man," he emphasized pointedly.

Ewan's face became thoughtful.

"Oh, Ewan, please let the doctor do what he thinks is best for you. Please!" begged the girl earnestly. "You cannot realize how important it all is."

Her earnestness betrayed her. Ewan turned his eyes on her with an inscrutable expression. The doctor's brows contracted and his fine lips pressed firmly together.

"Jove, Bessie, you talk as if you know something about the habits of this—ah—bug, or whatever it was," Ewan commented, his gaze scrutinizing his sister's flushed face. "How about it, sis?"

She threw a quick glance at the doctor for help and counsel.

"Your sister happened to see the—creature—that bit you," said the doctor slowly, "and described—it—to me. Do you wish to tell him, Bessie?"

The girl turned her back to them both, shuddering uncontrollably. Her voice was half smothered when she finally spoke.

"No, I can't tell him now. You know I can't. He would be furious with me. He wouldn't believe me," she almost whispered.

"Bessie!" reproached her brother sharply.

"Well, Ewan," the girl cried, whirling about to face him, her gentle face convulsed by the emotion induced by the fearful memory of that night, "if I cannot, myself, credit fully as yet the evidence of my own eyes, how can I expect you to?"

Ewan eyed her in silence. At last he said, his face moody: "There's something darned queer about this whole business. I don't understand it. I admit that. But I do know one thing: if I've been bitten by something venomous, and you, Dr. Armitage, believe you can heal the wound and stop the circulation of the poison through my system—well, I put myself unreservedly into your hands. Until," he added hastily, "until the wound is healed and the poison gone. Then I shall certainly expect an explanation of all this mystery. It seems very childish to me now."

Bessie had dropped her face into her hands and was crying softly.

"Don't, please, Bessie!" The doctor sprang to his feet and looked at her with all his heart plainly written on his face. "He shall be healed, I promise you. Don't worry, dear. He has put himself into my hands, and I can take care of him if my directions are followed with strict attention."

The girl finally managed to choke back her sobs of relief at her brother's decision. She raised her tear-stained face to meet Ewan's pluckily.

"Why, sis, I'd no idea you'd feel that way about it," said her twin, deeply touched by her sisterly solicitude. "Well, doctor, on with the dance! What's first on the docket?" Dr. Armitage's reply was wordless. He went to the door, opened it cautiously, peering outside beforehand. He leaned down and came back, barring the door behind him. His arms were full of blossoming sprays of wild roses.

"This is the best I can do tonight. They must go all over the window crevices in your brother's room," he directed, addressing Bessie with an appeal in his dark eyes to which she responded, although the oddity of his orders was stirring Ewan into a humorous mood.

"Is that part of the 'important treatment'?" inquired the artist, struggling to maintain his gravity, the absurdity of decorating his room with flowers as a precaution having affected his risibility.

"This is an important part of the precautions that we must take to prevent a further recurrence of infection," responded the doctor, his face so grave that the other man controlled himself for fear of stirring Dale Armitage to indignation. "Over the doorway here," he added, placing a long pink-blossomed spray over the lintel of the door that led out-of-doors from the larger room.

"Aren't you going to put something on my neck?" inquired Ewan with considerable curiosity.

The doctor gave him a long look. "It won't be necessary," he said finally. "That is, as long as you are wearing this," and he took from his pocket a rosary with a crucifix of silver.

"I'm not a Catholic," declared Ewan decidedly. "Why on Earth should I put that about my neck? It's absurd."

"It may be absurd to you," responded the doctor quietly, "but it is part—and a deeply serious part—of the necessary treatment. If you keep this crucifix close about your neck, Mr. Gillespie, that— Thing—which infected you will be unable to approach easily."

"Jove! Do you actually expect me to believe that?"

"I do not care whether you believe it or not," flashed the other man, "as long as you follow my orders to wear it."

"Oh, I suppose I shall have to, then," submitted Ewan, with unexpected meekness. "But I'll say I never thought I'd be wearing a Catholic emblem—"

"Is the cross any more Catholic than Protestant?" demanded the doctor sharply. "It is not the thing in itself. It is what hundreds of years of reverence and adoration from millions of human souls have made it. It is the visible emblem of that which has been the redemption of mankind from Evil, and as such, Evil flees it today because of its powerful occult influence, gathered through the ages from the loving worship of so many human hearts."

The doctor finished fastening the wild rose branches about Ewan's room.

"Now, Mr. Gillespie, if the windows and doors are kept tightly closed tonight, and that crucifix remains on your neck, I can guarantee that you will sleep well, waken refreshed and stronger—"

"And the wounds will heal, won't they?" eagerly interrupted the girl.

"And the wounds—in time—will heal," agreed the doctor. "But—"

"Ah, always there is a 'but'," the artist murmured, with an odd expression on his face as he fingered the rosary about his neck and stared at the garlands now decorating his sleeping quarters.

"In the meantime, Mr. Gillespie, you must agree not to see Mrs. Armitage alone," decreed the doctor, and with a quickly uplifted finger cut short Ewan's instant, indignant protest. "After the wounds have healed and I have explained to you, in her presence if necessary, the cause of them—you may make your own choice about seeing her further," he ended heavily in a dejected tone. "But that choice may spell tragedy to you," he added, grimly.

Ewan's eyes were on the doctor's face.

"Frankly," said he lightly, "my opinion is that you're off your head. But as Bessie insists—and I've promised—I'll keep to your orders. So I accept the added foolish condition, with its corollary that I may have the honor of seeing Mrs. Armitage later on, in her husband's presence," he laughed.

He turned on his heel and went into his room, closing the door without so little as a goodnight.

"Oh, Dale!"

Bessie was perilously close to tears again.

The doctor went to her, gently took her hands in his and held them quietly until it seemed to her that she could feel his strength pouring into her from his strong, cool fingers.

"Bessie, my dear, if your brother does not see Gretel privately until those wounds are healed, all will go well with him. But you," he ordered reluctantly, "must watch over him all night. She will try her utmost to impress her evil wishes upon his subjective mind, forcing him to tear off the crucifix I have placed about his neck, and even to pull down the protecting branches of the wild rose that I have put about his window and door, for she has this power over him now. As long as all remains as arranged, she cannot enter, bodily. Have you the courage to undertake this vigil?"

"Can't you stay?" she quavered, the whole horror of the prospective night weighing upon her spirits.

He shook his head in negation.

"No, brown girl, I cannot remain. I must return to her. In my own way I must also watch. I must keep her mind so occupied that she will be unable to concentrate upon your brother."

"Was she angry?" queried Bessie timidly.

He laughed, a short, grim laugh.

"Angry! If that could describe it, Bessie! She made a threat which I hardly think she will carry out. If she does," he said huskily, "God would have to be especially merciful to all three of us here!"

Bessie's fingers trembled in his. Her hazel eyes glazed with inward terror. "Dale, you terrify me! What—what do you mean?"

"My dear, if she gets the opportunity to carry out her threat, an opportunity I don't intend she shall have, then it will be time enough for me to tell you what I mean. Until then, do not open the door until morning breaks full," he warned impressively. "Nor a window. And keep awake, for Ewan's sake. Do not leave him out of your sight for a single minute."

Bessie, white to the lips, nodded acquiescence.

Chapter 9
On the Wings of the Wind

As she barred the door when the doctor left, Bessie found herself shaking with nervous chills. All her life she had been protected; an old-fashioned home girl. Never had she been separated from her twin brother as she was now, in spirit. Depressing and terrifying was the thought that she must spend that entire night virtually alone, with an evil something hovering near with malicious intent, the outworking of which she could not foresee. Only the reflection that Dale Armitage would be thinking of her, struggling from his own place to protect Ewan and herself, comforted her, for she had much confidence in his superior knowledge and ability to ward off this pressing evil.

Hardly had the doctor gone than Bessie heard her brother stirring in his room. She flew to the communicating door and opened it, with a light but imperative tap. Ewan stood at the window, pulling down the sprays of wild roses which the doctor had placed about it. On the floor lay the rosary, where he must have tossed it after tearing it from his neck. At his sister's involuntary cry of apprehension and warning, Ewan turned and faced her. She shrank sickly at the revelation of that hard, far-away gaze that seemed to pass through her and out—out—beyond the cabin walls.

"Ewan! What are you doing? You promised!" she cried.

As she called his name, the artist shuddered slightly. By slow degrees his eyes became more normal. He moved his head so that his gaze rested on his sister's solicitous face. Then it passed her and went, as if drawn irresistibly, to the window.

"Jove!" The ejaculation was jerked convulsively from his pale lips. "Bessie! Bessie! Am I mad? Or do you see it, too?"

His sister sprang across the room to his side. She had had a moment's terrible hallucination; or so she explained it to herself, for she feared to admit it was anything more substantial than a purely mental image that had all at once flattened chalky face against the window, with parted crimson lips drawn back tightly against red gums and pointed, shining white teeth. And those horridly gleaming eyes! Plashing with ruby glints! The evil smile!

"Come away from that window, Ewan!" she screamed, grasping her brother's arm in sheer panic.

The artist retreated slowly, but his eyes were glued to the panes, and in them once more that far-away look began to grow. He moved like a person in a trance.

Bessie pulled at him frantically. Then she leaned down, picked up the rosary and tried to put it about his neck, a gesture he vaguely but ineffectually repulsed. She had the final satisfaction of seeing the sacred emblem slip down over his heart.

He sighed deeply, then, and removed his eyes from the window. Still in that dazed manner he groped his way back to his cot and let himself slip supinely upon it, his sister watching meantime in an agony of apprehension lest that ghastly countenance that had seemed to flash against the windowpane should once more glare in upon them.

"I'm—sleepy," drawled the artist.

He closed heavy lids, seemingly falling quickly into a deep sleep.

Bessie, although she shrank from approaching the window, crossed the room again and picked up the wild rose sprays. She replaced them in as nearly the same positions as the doctor had. Then she went into the living room for a hammer and some nails, determined to tack a piece of burlap securely over the window, to put a permanent stop to such hallucinations. This accomplished, she felt much more comfortable, and with Ewan's door open so that she could watch him from her seat by the table, where she purposed to sit and read, Bessie settled herself for her long night vigil.

The alarm-clock ticked sedately on the table before her, until its little black hands passed 3 o'clock. A penetrating cold, strangely out of place on a summer night, began to chill her to the marrow. And she found herself attacked by fits of yawning, and a deep longing for sleep. At that, she rose and began to prepare hot coffee, to ward off that overwhelming impulse to throw herself on her cot and let herself slip off into slumber.

As she stood over the bubbling saucepan, watching the boiling water rise around the edges and overflow the island of coffee in its midst, a sudden roaring in the forest aisles startled her into frozen stillness. It was as if all the trees were suddenly shouting together; a tumult almost incredible to have come without previous warning into the quiet peace of the night. And in the midst of that terrible, portentous sound there was borne to Bessie's straining ears a wailing cry of eerie omen that sent her staggering back against the table, clutching at the edge of it to support her trembling body.

"Help—help—help!" wailed that shrilling voice, and the cry was a woman's, and it came from a soul in the final throes of some intolerable agony.

The roaring in the forest trees grew with noticeable steadiness into a fearful uproar that seemed the voice of a tremendous volume of blasting wind, but in spite of all this racket the little cabin seemed to stand in the midst of a mighty calm, for there was no whistling of that tremendous air movement around its sturdy walls. Yet a terrible and penetrating cold came pushing through every crack and crevice. And ever above the booming of that mysterious force, whatever it was that swelled thundering among the forest giants, shrilled with distinct and horrisonous significance that woman's cry for help.

Although the blood seemed congealing about her slowly heating heart, Bessie Gillespie's first thought was for her brother, for that this cry upon the mounting larum of the forest was a portent of impending evil she felt instinctively. At her hasty glance about, she saw that the wild rose spray over Ewan's door had slipped off and disappeared. She remembered that she had caught them, all up in her perturbation of spirit and had put them about the window, that spray, probably, with the others. She ran now to the living room door and pulled down the branch above it. This she pushed into position over the lintel of the door leading to her brother's room, and heaved a deep sigh of relief as she saw him apparently in a heavy sleep, the beads of the rosary just in sight about his neck, and the window protected, as she had last arranged it.

Now there came a wild rapping at the cabin door. A frantic pounding of fists upon the sturdy wood. Then the noisy moaning as of a woman's ultimate clamoring appeal, wordless in its stress of emotion.

essie trembled where she stood, indecision whirling her mentally this way and that. Ewan, if she could believe the doctor's word, was more or less safe as long as the wild rose sprays and the crucifix remained in place; unless he wakened, tore them down, or emerged from the room which just now was his one refuge. She told herself that if that shouting tumult of the forest had not wakened him, nothing else could.

She knew that she could not refuse admittance to that poor soul moaning without her door. There were bears and wildcats in the woods, so Amity Dam folk had told Ewan. And the cold was biting more and more cruelly in spite of the fire the girl had made in the stove to boil her coffee. Suppose a wild animal should attack some poor night wanderer outside her very door; in the morning she might find the half-devoured body, the picked bones…Her dark hair almost stood on end at this obnoxious thought; she felt that she could not, in the name of common humanity, ignore that cry in the night.

With a swelling prayer for protection and guidance, she lifted the bar from the door. Simultaneously, it burst inward, bringing with it all the roar of the furious forest giants, and bearing upon that almost tangible booming the form of a woman that came sweeping upon the startled girl as if actually carried into the cabin by the force of the wild gust. And as Bessie retreated in involuntary dismay—although to her increasing bewilderment not a breath of air seemed to infringe upon the stillness of the room's atmosphere— the din and hubbub was gone as suddenly as it had arisen. The cabin door slammed shut as if sucked back by the retreating of those mysterious and potent forces that had been invoked for her own fell purpose by Gretel Armitage, who uncovered her flaxen hair with a quick gesture that flung her enveloping mantle aside imperiously.

"You!" gasped Bessie, retreating toward Ewan's door in an attitude of unconscious guardianship, her arms out, her palms spread against this unexpected and unwelcome visitor.

Gretel smiled in a superior way, disclosing sharp white teeth between her ruby lips, which she touched delicately with her red tongue in a manner almost animal, wakening apprehensive shudders in that other woman who stood watching and waiting for the visitor's next move.

"Didn't you expect me?" murmured Gretel sweetly. "Surely you must have known that I would come again—and again—after your brother brought me in here in his arms, against his heart," she stabbed softly, subtly.

Bessie's hazel eyes darkened with anger and fear.

"It is abominable of you to have returned," she enunciated finally, speaking with careful precision, and standing before Ewan's threshold with firmness, while her heart beat heavily and her soul cried out for courage and help. "Was there any reason why you should beat upon my door as you did, when you have a home of your own to shelter you?"

"A home of my own?" said the doctor's wife, with an indescribably bitter accent. "Girl, I have no home. Home—home is where the heart is, they say. My heart has been trampled upon until its sweetness has been turned to fury and resentment. There is no place where I can rest my aching heart, you brown thing," she cried with a sudden flash of such concentrated venom that Bessie shrank hastily backward.

"What brought you here?" demanded the girl, summoning all her courage, and throwing back her shoulders pluckily.

"What brought me here? Your brother, my dear, of whom I am very fond," replied the doctor's wife, with an oddly surreptitious glance into the room beyond Bessie. "Why all those flowers? Is that interior decorating idea yours?"

"Your husband put those sprays there," replied the girl steadily. "And you know why. You know why my brother is not himself just now. He is protected, thanks to your husband. You shall not have him again, as you did the other night. Dale knows all about it, and he will see that my brother is kept in safety."

"'Dale'?" repeated Gretel, musingly. "So you are having a little intrigue of your own, you demure brown thing? I might tell you that if you let my husband alone, I'd let your brother alone, but—but I intend to have your brother for my own. Already he is half mine," she said, leaning forward with lifted eyebrows, as if in pretty confidential mood. "Tonight—or some other night—will be all the same to me. I can wait, Bessie Gillespie. He will be entirely mine, when I find the right opportunity, as find it I shall. And that is a promise," she added, scarlet lips drawing into a straight, uncompromising line. "Now, my dear, for you—"

At the flickering red lights in those flashing blue eyes, Bessie felt herself grow faint. There was something irresistibly alluring, if terrible, emanating from the doctor's wife, as she stood without moving from the spot where the forest forces had brought her; it stirred at the very roots of the girl's hair until she could feel each separate hair stiffening on her prickling scalp. She clutched at the doorway on either side, hazel eyes wide, fixed upon the unwavering, snakelike gaze of Gretel Armitage. The strange hypnotic orbs of the doctor's wife did not move from Bessie's strained face; over Gretel's countenance there began to play a subtle expression of gratification and unsuppressed amusement.

"Oh, Bessie, you are so simple and so easy to handle!" gurgled the doctor's wife softly. "After all, it will be amusing to take you first. Ewan can wait for my kisses; he cannot get away from me, for he has tasted them once. You are losing yourself, my plump brown maid—you are falling into the abysses of my eyes, that are drowning you in flames of dizzy rapture—" The voice droned on, sending humming tones through Bessie's unhappy, unwilling ears.

All at once, brusk and imperative, came Gretel's command. "Put out that light on the table, my dear," she said sharply. "It would only draw my furious husband here after me, and—ah, how I love the enveloping darkness," she ended in a lower tone. "Do as I tell you, Bessie. You have saved your brother for tonight. I shall not bother him just now, for you will do very nicely in his stead. Let him grow strong again; all the better for me!" Her eerie laugh sounded like the intolerable resonance of silver bells, which rang—and rang— and rang—in Bessie's ears.

The girl stirred in the doorway and moved away from it slowly. Her arms fell limply at her sides. Her dazed eyes were drawn powerfully to those fixed, redly flashing orbs of the other woman, who stood smiling confidently in the middle of the living room.

Through Bessie's whole body a pleasant languor crept, a kind of voluptuous pleasure in the urging of her body forward under the will of that other, a releasing of responsibility that gave her a sense of freedom, almost sweet.

"Come, rosy Bessie! Put out the light," droned Gretel's achingly penetrating voice. "You have hated me, but you shall yet love me with every drop of your blood." She laughed softly, terribly. "Come, and when we are in the enveloping darkness I shall put my arms tightly about you, lovely little plump brown thing that you are. Oh, it will be much pleasanter than Dale's kisses, when you sink into delicate faintness under my lips, I promise you! Put out the light, my dear, so that you may come the more quickly and surely into my arms! Oh, you will thrill—from head to foot—with delicious tremblings. Ah, Bessie, I love you already, for you are almost mine. When you are completely mine, I shall love you very tenderly—and you will come to me and offer me everything you have to give, my dear! Come—come—I long to have you of your own free will—it will be more delicious to have it so—little brown thing!"

The voice was languorous, thrillingly sweet and penetrating. Gretel leaned forward, arms outstretched, long fingers beckoning. Her ruby lips smiled with a terrible significance. Her white, pointed teeth flashed as she touched them with her tongue. About her shoulders tumbled that writhing mass of flaxen hair that had veiled Ewan's face as his head lay on her lap that other night.

Bessie took an involuntary step forward, drawn by Gretel's encouraging smile. She moved dazed-like across the room to the table, stretched out her hand, turned down the wick. The dim flame still flickered and smoldered.

"Blow it out!" commanded Gretel's voice, in harsh impatience, a panicky haste running in undertone through every accent. "Hurry! I can hear Dale's feet trampling through the forest! Hurry, Bessie, or you will not taste tonight what I have promised you! The thrill— the ecstasy—of my kisses—"

Bessie turned her face toward the smoldering light of the lamp, her lips pursed to blow out the flame. As she turned, a shout from the clearing startled her from her half-trance into her normal con-sciousness. She followed out the intended action under the impetus of Gretel's imperative order, but as the flame died, she knew what awaited her, and from her lips went a shrill, wailing cry of terrible helplessness, as she found herself gripped firmly in Gretel's arms in the darkness.

Gretel's lips were moistly, horribly, pressing upon her shrinking flesh.

The darkness grew Stygian, heavy, oppressive. In it Bessie strag-gled weakly to push those sharp white teeth away, even if her flesh were torn badly in her effort to escape that impending doom. She realized her futility. The atmosphere was supercharged with malicious triumph. Evil reigned supreme.

Gretel's panting breath came hotly against the struggling girl's throat. Gretel's white teeth met with a click—

"Dale!" sobbed Bessie.

Consciousness left the agonized girl as a sharp pain at her throat apprized her that her battle was lost.

Gretel was chuckling horribly in the dark.

Chapter 10
Rescue

There were swimming, swirling clouds of gray and black, flecked with ruby points of dancing light. There were humming, droning sounds, broken in upon by staccato sharpnesses of speech, cracked by emotion into short but pregnant words. There was an aching of muscles, as if she had received repeated blows.

Bessie Gillespie struggled back into consciousness that did not for some time seem normal to her, for it was a strange and mysterious scene upon which her hazel eyes finally opened, half dazed.

She lay where Gretel Armitage must have flung her drooping body when the doctor had burst into the cabin with his electric flash; stretched in crumpled relaxation upon the board flooring, bruised and aching.

The doctor had stood his flashlight upon the floor in order to give light and at the same time leave his hands free for whatever action he found it necessary to take. The circles of light from the torch illuminated the ceiling and but dimly gave relief to the white faces of the doctor and his wife as they confronted each other.

Gretel was obviously at bay. Her blue eyes were deep spheres of strange ruby fire. Between snarling red lips shone the pointed sharpness of her glistening white teeth. The expression upon that fair face was the look of a thwarted fiend. Her hands, lifted on either side of that terrible countenance, were like the talons of some unclean bird of prey. She crouched and cringed, as if in dire fear and fury.

The doctor, on the contrary, stood upright, his deep eyes glowing with what seemed to the wondering Bessie a strangely comforting radiance. His melancholy face was wearier than ever; sadder than ever; as if he had all at once found yet another burden to lay upon his soul. But behind that sadness a something surged and swelled and broke out in his few words that seemed charged with a more than ordinary pregnancy and power. It was as if he felt within himself that which would bear him on to triumph over evil, and feeling it, he had no fear for the outcome.

Painfully drawing herself into a sitting posture, Bessie began to understand the actual words passing between those two, even though she could not seem to gain any real insight into their esoteric meaning.

"I didn't mean any harm," Gretel whined, those clawlike fingers curling and uncurling, a demoniacal expression on her face, as she slyly watched the doctor's every movement. "I would only have taken—a little—and you had frightened me—and I needed—strength."

"You deliberately stole out of the home that in your better moments you had chosen as your earthly prison," charged the doctor sternly. "You deliberately came here, in a spirit of revenge against me, to hurt innocent people in the hope that this would hurt me most of all."

"But she isn't hurt," eagerly exclaimed his wife in a croaking voice, those clutching talons moving eerily about her face, throwing strangely writhing shadows across it.

"Because I came in time," retorted the doctor harshly, no pity showing in his grim face. "Another second, and you would have added this poor girl to your list of victims," he accused bitterly.

Bessie's hand went instinctively to her throat. Her fingers, examining the smooth surface with gingerly delicacy, found little roughnesses where those pointed teeth had met. She paled and listened strainedly, her fingers protectively over those tiny, terrible, ominous wounds, which she feared the doctor had not seen.

"But you didn't give me time," almost complained Gretel, in a peevish whine. The interlacing shadows of her clawlike fingers moved more and more like dark serpents' trails over her writhing face. "I am still parched—"

"Enough, you fiend!" commanded the doctor sharply. "There is no repentance possible for you, is there, Gretel? No remorse? Well, you will go back to the lodge now, and after I have seen to these two people I shall return, and after that there will be less freedom of action for you, since you are no longer to be trusted. Make no mistake," he added quickly, as a kind of twisted smile drew up his wife's vivid lips, "when I am with you I am protected in ways that do not concern you. You see, my dear Gretel, I take no chances," said he coldly.

"Oh! You wish to make me a perpetual prisoner! You, whose fault it is that I am as I am!" she shrilled, drawing herself upright at last. "Why don't you kill me, and drive a stake through my heart, and cut off my head, and be done with it, once for all?"

The doctor regarded her impersonally as she raged.

"Because that kind of thing isn't being done, my dear Gretel," he responded dryly after a moment's silence.

"That's not the true reason, Dale, and you know it isn't," she screamed back. "It's because even in your hard heart there's remorse for what you did to an innocent girl who loved you! That's why you don't dare do now what you think you will when I die! Ah—but you won't then."

Her face grew sly and narrow with cunning; the redly flashing eyes peered from beneath lowered lashes. A hissing little laugh that sent sick shudders over the listening Bessie came in gusts through the drawn red lips.

"What do you mean? Are you trying to threaten me again?" demanded Dr. Armitage. "If you are, I'll have this thing out with you here and now, for I'll not permit a Thing like you let loose upon the world while I can prevent it," he declared with definiteness.

"They'd send you to the electric chair," whispered his wife, trembling with some secret mirth. "You wouldn't dare—"

"That is sufficient!" cried out the doctor, his voice raised with high authority. "Go home, Gretel! Go to your room. Sit down, think—"

"She's coming to herself," interrupted Gretel, those sly eyes now on Bessie's wide hazel orbs. "Did you hear what I said, Bessie Gillespie? Well, I'll say more. I'm sorry Dale came when he did, and the next time I come to you, Bessie, I won't come so gently," croaked the doctor's wife venomously.

"Oh!" cried Bessie, appealing to Dale with anxious face.

"This man whom you think so wonderful, Bessie, is the cause of my—of my being—what I am." Gretel broke into wild sobbing, beating the air with clawlike fingers while great tears tumbled down her working face. "He can't deny it," she choked out. "I was an innocent, unsuspecting girl, and he—"

"Oh, my God!" cried the baited physician in a kind of dogged despair. "Will you go home, Gretel?"

"Is it your fault? Tell her that, at least!" snarled his wife, tears and sobs ceasing with as much abruptness as they had begun.

There was a moment's silence. Bessie, sitting on the floor, her eyes going from one to the other, now sought the doctor's face, and his gaze, deep and melancholy, rested on her questioning but trustful countenance. At last he spoke, heavily:

"It was my fault, but—"

"You hear that?" Gretel shrieked exultantly. "He made me the Thing I have become, and now he wants to shut me up in one room until I die," she relapsed whiningly, and cringed before the darkness of her husband's lowering eyes.

Dale went across the room and extended his hands to Bessie, helping her to her feet and then to a chair. He scratched a match and soon the cheery, comforting yellow glow of the kerosene lamp brightened the eerie shadows in the room, so that what had happened in that dancing half-light, what had been said even, appeared all at once a fantasy.

"I'm going," said Mrs. Armitage shortly, to her husband. "I'm—I'm sorry—in a way—for what has occurred tonight." Her eyes went to Bessie's still pale face in a peculiar fashion.

"Gretel, to hear you say you are sorry," began the doctor, when she spoke again, hastily.

"I was too precipitate," she murmured, hatefully. "I should have waited for a better opportunity," and she laughed vindictively.

"Go home, Gretel, before you anger me beyond my power of control," commanded the doctor, pointing to the door.

"You trust me to go alone, Dale? Aren't you afraid I may—?"

"You dare not!" he snapped at her sharply.

A wild cachinnation pealed from the red lips. The pointed little tongue moistened Gretel's mouth, protruding from the white pointed teeth with the lightning rapidity of a serpent's forked one. Her shoulders shook with her ugly mirth, its malignant undertones making Bessie shudder anew.

"So I am to go on home, with the agreeable prospect ahead of me of being immured for life?" said she. "And I am to leave my husband here with his new, his latest, fancy?" she finished scathingly, stabbing at Bessie with her light, pointed words. "Well, my dear, you are welcome to him, if you want him. He'll be mine, eventually. And in the meantime, I'd far rather have your complaisant, unsophisticated brother," she finished, with another peal of strange, eerie laughter, as she went out into the night through the open cabin door. "But do not forget. Dale isn't too clever for me, yet," she called back, menacingly.

The sound of her feet as they crunched dry branches under them, went across the clearing. Then silence, and a low cry from the night.

"I forgot. The stream," explained the doctor in a low voice. "I'll be back, Bessie. I must carry her across the running water."

When the doctor returned, the girl asked curiously, "If she must be carried across the stream, how did she come this evening, from the lodge?"

"Bessie, she called upon certain elemental forces in nature that are bound, under given conditions, to serve her. That much she has gained from her study of Black Art. And these forces drew down from the icy north a bitter, biting, freezing wind. Gretel crossed that stream because the surface was frozen."

A stirring in Ewan's room called for their attention.

"Did she get in there?" demanded the doctor briefly.

Bessie shook her head.

"No. But he got up once and began pulling down the rose sprays. He threw the rosary on the floor. And we saw a terrible face"—she shuddered—"peering in at the window."

"That was her astral projection," the doctor explained. "I called her back when I got to the lodge."

He tiptoed to Ewan's side and looked down upon the young artist, whose breath came slowly and regularly. He was nodding with satisfaction when he went back to the living

"He'll come along nicely now," said he with a relieved sigh. "After this night's escapade Gretel will find herself so closely confined that she will be unable to escape my vigilance again," grimly. "Now let me see your throat, Bessie. She said she had not had time to injure you, but I cannot take her word when she is fiend-inspired." He pushed the girl's chin up and with the electric torch in one hand made a close and careful examination of her neck. "It's all right, dear. She tore the skin a bit with her sharp teeth, but there's been no blood drawn as yet; the wounds are perfectly dry. We'll put a bit of iodine on the wound, to avoid ordinary infection."

"Then I'm not like Ewan?" faltered the girl.

The doctor shook a decisive negative. "Bessie, I came here, guided by providence, in the very nick of time. A fraction of a second later would have been too late. Good Lord, what a terrible mess it is!" he ended, with a heavy sigh that was almost a groan.

Bessie put her soft little hands to his working face and held his cheeks a moment in that tender, comforting pressure.

The doctor turned his face gently until his lips touched one caressing hand. Then he picked up the flashlight and turned toward the still open door.

"I must get back, brown girl, and have it out with Gretel," he sighed. "She agreed to some degree of restraint, but she has tasted human blood too often, and now she is harder to control. However, when daylight comes she is usually amenable to reason, and I hope to arrange matters so she cannot emerge without my knowledge. Try to sleep, brown girl. Your brother is safe now, and so are you. Unless," he added darkly, "Gretel carried out her threat."

"Good night, dear Dale," said Bessie quietly, as she barred the door behind him.

Sleep she could not. The night's terrible happenings had been too nerve-disturbing for her to relax sufficiently for sleep. Doze she did, a little: conscious always of her surroundings and quickly responsive to the slightest sound from her brother's room.

And so the darkness passed slowly away, until gray dawn began to tear down the night's dark defenses, that the morning sun might pour its cheering rays through the forest glades.

And in the half-light of dawn came the consciousness that for hours there had been a steady sound of marching footsteps outside the cabin. With the realization, Bessie came into full wakefulness and ran to the window to see who was without.

Like a sentinel on guard, Dr. Armitage paced hack and forth before the cabin door, his head hanging wearily, his whole attitude one of resignation and despair.

Chapter 11
Ewan Demands an Explanation

Behind her, Ewan came staring, just roused from a sleep that had done him much good, for his haggard face looked rested and his eyes were brighter, clearer, than they had been since the night of the big thunderstorm.

"Am I seeing straight, sis?" demanded the artist incredulously. "Is our good neighbor standing guard to protect us from the mysterious bug, or am I dreaming?"

The intuition of something not quite right gripped Bessie as she looked out at the doctor's robust figure, slightly bowed now as he walked with head down, as if heavily burdened by secret troubles.

"It's Dr. Armitage, Ewan. Watching over both of us. I'm going to ask him to have some coffee with us. Ewan"—her voice was serious as she drew back from the window to confront her amused, contemptuous brother—"you may never know how much you owe him, so I'm going to beg you to be pleasant to him."

"I'll be pleasant to him," agreed Ewan shortly, "but what he's done for me I'm going to find out. I don't intend to be kept in the dark like a baby, Bessie. Now that I've had a good night's sleep, I feel more like myself, and"—his hands went to his throat—"and it seems the poisonous bites about which both of you were so alarmed are getting better. I don't feel all drawn up into them, the way I did last night."

"Due entirely to Dr. Armitage's precautions, no matter how silly they seemed to you," said his sister, gravely.

"Due, dear Bessie, to the iodine you put on the bites before he arrived," asseverated the young artist lightly. "However, let's be nice to our neighbor, who's evidently been standing guard over us like a soldier on duty."

Ewan unbarred the cabin door, opened it, and hailed the doctor with a friendly intonation that brought a lighter look to Dale's melancholy face.

"Come in and have coffee with us, neighbor. My sister says you've been watching over us all night, and as I'm not distributing medals this morning you rate a hot drink, at least."

Dr. Armitage came into the cabin slowly, his footsteps heavy and his manner that of a man weighed down by apprehension. He took a chair and looked dully about the room as Bessie started breakfast preparations.

"It was kind of you to come back, Dale," said she, cutting bread deftly.

"I only hope I didn't alarm you," said the doctor absently.

"I didn't know until this morning," she confessed.

"Then you weren't disturbed after I left last night?" he queried with a quick glance at Ewan.

"I must have slept like the proverbial log all night," Ewan declared. "Due, of course, to the floral decorations," he added, with a quirk to his lips.

The doctor passed over this innuendo as a trifle of no importance.

"The main thing is that neither of you were disturbed. You see," and he hesitated, with a troubled gathering of his dark brows, "you see, my—Mrs. Armitage—didn't return to the lodge last night."

"What? Was she here last night?" cried Ewan, marveling at such an indiscretion on Gretel's part.

Bessie's face was white and she steadied her hand by a visible effort so as not to spill the coffee she was straining off.

"Where can she be?" she murmured tremblingly.

The doctor turned a ghastly face to hers. His eyes were burning in their sockets with the misery he was experiencing. He ignored the artist as if at that moment there were but two people in the world; himself and Bessie.

"My dear," said he very simply, "my dear, Gretel has gone to carry out her mad and wicked threat. I should not have trusted her out of my sight. I should have known that she would take that last desperate means of revenging herself upon me before I locked her up permanently. There can be no safety in this world or the next for your brother, and perhaps for us, until we can find her body, and do to her what I had to do to that pitiful baby that I told you about."

His voice broke. He leaned forward, resting his face on his cupped hands.

Bessie put down the coffee-pot abruptly, uncaring that it marked the spotless oil-cloth of the kitchen table with black soot. She laid her hands softly on the doctor's head and stood in perfect silence, her hot tears of sympathy dropping on his hair.

"Are you people out of your minds?" questioned the artist, after staring at this scene with astonished face. "Bessie, you ought to be ashamed of yourself. That man is married," said Ewan's angry whisper. "Don't you understand?"

"I understand perfectly, Ewan. Don't be angry, dear. You—you see, you don't understand everything as I do. Poor Dale!" and she did not remove her tender hands.

"Jove! This is a ridiculous and disgraceful situation!" The artist, conveniently forgetting, manlike, his own derelictions of so recent occurrence, turned the volume of his indignation upon the physician. "Dr. Armitage, you are a married man, and you permit—you encourage—my sister to—to—" he stuttered indignantly.

Dr. Armitage lifted his face from his palms.

"On the surface, Gillespie, you are right to be indignant with me, but as your sister just told you, you are aware of nothing that lies beneath this situation. If you did, in ever so small a manner, dream of it, you would not ask her to remove her comforting, gracious hands from my weary head," he said dejectedly.

Ewan looked from one to the other, puzzled.

"There's something darned queer about the whole situation, I'll tell the world. Out with it! If I'm to be so complaisant, I may as well know the reason why. I'm not a child, to be kept in the dark when there's anything important going on," he growled testily.

Bessie continued to stroke the doctor's hair until he put up his hands, took hers, and drew them down on one shoulder, where he held them under one of his.

"Gillespie, I have every reason to believe that your body and soul are, from now on, in such deadly peril that I hesitate to state the conditions from which this danger arises, for fear you will not believe me, and will refuse to be guided by my knowledge of what it may be best to do under these conditions."

"All this you've said before, and I'm feeling fine this morning," returned the artist truculently. "Whatever bit me"—and he grimaced at the recollection of his weakness of the previous day—"evidently poisoned me a bit, but I'm okay now. So I can hardly apprehend any very immediate danger," dryly.

"Ewan! You're acting like a stupid schoolboy!" flashed his sister hotly. "It's just plain ignorance that makes you so cocksure. If you— if you'd gone through—with what I have," and her voice broke into a quaver, "you'd listen to what Dale has to say."

"What has happened to you, Bessie?" demanded her brother, going to her and putting his arms tenderly about her, drawing her away from the doctor and to himself.

Bessie's eyes questioned the physician, who nodded assent wearily.

"**L**ast night, Ewan, Gretel came here again," the girl began, speaking with difficulty as the horror of that night came back vividly to her memory. "She—she made me put out the light—and she—she tried to bite my throat as she did yours—"

"Bessie!" He shook her violently. "For God's sake, stop talking such nonsense! Good Lord, Armitage, is she serious?"

"Your sister is very well poised nervously, or she'd not even be able to speak of last night's happenings," declared the doctor, forcibly. "That is, without breaking down. Let me tell the rest. It's entirely too hard for her. She's had a grilling experience."

"But she said—Gretel—bit her throat? And mine. Why?"

"For the same reason," steadily replied the physician, rising and confronting the young man, who held his sister's head on his shoulder comfortingly.

"She—she—bit—me?" puzzled the artist stupidly. "Pardon me, but did I really hear you aright? Your wife—bit me?" He disengaged one arm from Bessie's shoulders to touch his throat, a strange look on his face. "Why—tell me why—your wife should—bite me? It—it sounds—like comic opera or something."

The doctor shook his hands in the air with a desperate gesture.

"Good God, man, can't you see that it is almost impossible to credit? Well, if you insist, she punctured your neck so that she could draw out your blood, for which she was thirsting, Gillespie."

Ewan turned Bessie's head back with a lightning gesture of fury. He pushed up the girl's chin gently but determinedly, and stared at her white throat, marred by two tiny punctures. Then he groaned aloud and caught her to him again, hiding her face on his shoulder.

"Then your wife is insane!" he croaked, horror-stricken. "I—who—would have—dreamed it!"

"You thought her a martyr and me a brutally jealous husband, of course," said the doctor patiently. "That was to have been expected. It is her role, and mine, as she makes them out."

"But why should she want to suck my blood?" asked the artist, distastefully.

"You see, Bessie?" exclaimed the doctor in a despairing tone. "If I tell him the whole awful truth, he will refuse to believe me."

Bessie raised her head and looked into her brother's eyes.

"Ewan, Gretel is a—a vampire."

"A vampire? Vampires are bats, sis."

She shook her head vigorously. "No, Ewan, not all of them. There are some wretched human beings who so thirst for human blood—"

"Be careful, my dear, of what you are saying," warned Ewan.

"I tell you, Gretel is a vampire. She nearly drained you of blood the other night. She made sure that you were asleep, and she thought I was, too. But I saw her!" cried the girl wildly.

Ewan let her go from his arms, backed off, and slumped into a chair, speechless for a moment.

"She's crazy. That's all," he pronounced with finality.

"No, Gillespie, she isn't," disputed the doctor. "She's as well poised and as sane as you or I."

"And you told me I'd been bitten by something that might ruin me body and soul!" disgustedly.

"It is true. An awful fate awaits you, unless—"

Ewan interrupted. "And this awful fate?" he queried with an assumption of bored attention.

"And that fate is, Gillespie, that you are even now at her beck and call, unless constantly guarded by occult means. It is that when she has had her fill of your blood, and your body dies because it is quite, quite drained, you yourself will become a wandering night thing, that cannot rest in peace even in the arms of Death, but must forever go on—undead—infecting those whom you love, as Gretel infected you."

Ewan stood up. He was colorless. His eyes were blazing.

"Bessie, do you believe this folderol?" he demanded between set teeth.

"Dale says it is so," began the girl.

The doctor gave a grieved exclamation. "So you, too, have turned against me? Well, God has evidently decreed that I must carry my burden alone. And somewhere in the woods is hidden the body of what was once Gretel Armitage," he said solemnly. "It is my bounden duty to find that body and so do to it that the Evil which now animates it can no longer move it to obey its behests. Little as you may believe it, Gillespie, your own life in the hereafter depends entirely upon whether I am able to find her body," declared he in measured accents.

"How do you know she is dead?" demanded the artist truculently.

"Because she has frequently threatened to kill herself, in order to be freer to carry out her wicked designs," answered the doctor with marked and gentle patience.

"Why should she kill herself?" pursued Ewan.

"Because only by passing through the portals of Death can she gain the freedom which I denied her earthly body, at her own request."

"Still I do not understand."

"I see that I must tell you the whole story from the very beginning," said the doctor thoughtfully.

Ewan sat down with an air of patient resignation, but triumph shone in his eyes. At last the doctor was forced to yield and tell the fairytales with which he had been trying to stuff Bessie, Ewan told himself scornfully.

"Coffee, Bess," said he prosaically. "Have some coffee, doctor, before you begin. Now go to it! No interruptions."

Chapter 12
The Dead That Wakened

"It began in Munich," said the doctor. "In 1923. I'd gone there after the war, to assist in special researches bearing upon certain strange outbreaks of ghoulism in a number of adjacent hamlets. To explain my being asked to help our former enemies in this work, I may say that my studies and research along occult lines had given me sufficient material for a small pamphlet on the sporadic prevalence among peoples of a certain type of mental development, of vampirism and lycanthropy. This booklet had come to the attention of a well-known German savant, Adolf Himmbeeren, in translated form, and he sent for me at the request of his confreres, who believed me better versed along occult lines than they.

"Professor Himmbeeren took me directly into the bosom of his family with the utmost hospitality, placing at my disposal all the splendid resources of his library and laboratory, of which I at once took full advantage. I found many books—in German, which rather retarded my reading, for with that language I was familiar only in its more colloquial terms—which opened vistas of weird and bizarre thought before my mental vision, and into these I delved, with the gracious assistance of the professor's charming motherless child, a lovely blonde girl, named—Gretel."

Bessie breathed quicker, leaning against the table toward him, hazel eyes hungrily on his face, her strained attention plainly hanging on every word. The artist sat up in his chair, his brow slightly drawn as he regarded the doctor with hard scrutiny,

"Gretel," repeated the doctor slowly. "Gretel Himmbeeren. She seemed just a lovely slip of an innocent girl, and imperceptibly I came to lean upon her quick, intuitive grasp of the esoteric subjects I was studying, for her command of English was superb. She spoke it without accent, as she did French, Italian, Spanish, and Russian. She was, in a word, an accomplished linguist, and I soon found that her knowledge of occult works was fully equal to my own. Due to her curiosity for the black magic which has been the bane of ignorant searchers and would-be magicians (she explained her interest on the ground of preparation to work against this widespread but unacknowledged evil), I found myself rapidly acquiring a fund of information from the archives not only of Germany, but of Italy, France, Spain, and Russia.

"I was naturally grateful to this young girl for her profound interest in my research, and her enthusiastic cooperation whenever I stood in need of it, but there was not the slightest emotional slant in my feelings toward her. This was something she was unable to grasp; to her my gratitude, fervently expressed, was but the froth bubbling up from some deeper emotion, and she unhappily permitted herself to be carried away by her confidence in her own judgment, and became deeply—only too deeply—involved toward me in her affectional life.

"I became aware of this first when her father fell ill, and we had to take turns watching at his bedside, for his long delving into the occult and his early ignorance of the proper methods for protecting himself against malign influences had laid him open to certain very evil—" Dale stopped hesitatingly, then went on: "Suffice it to say that he was afraid to be alone, and feared also to be left with a nurse unversed in the occult. Both Gretel and I knew how to protect him while he slept, and only when one of us was present would he relax. It was during those night watches that Gretel's passion burst its bounds, plainly showing that she had long lost an impersonal attitude toward me. I had maintained mine toward her so scrupulously, even in my slightest thought, that her sudden revelation came to me as a distinct shock."

"And you, a physician, were totally unprepared for the consequences of propinquity," observed Ewan, scathingly, lips scornful.

"I've seen you treat your models with exactly that entire lack of personal feeling, Ewan," cried Bessie reproachfully. "You've been so submerged in your work that you've forgotten they were human beings even."

Ewan colored slightly.

"Your rebuke is a just one, sis," he admitted. "Pardon me, doctor, for my interruption. Perhaps I was hasty."

The doctor's dark eyes grew brighter. He even smiled.

"You are very excusable, Gillespie. And please let me assure you that I am honest when I say that to me it was both startling and disconcerting to have Gretel let down the safe bars of impersonality and open the windows of her soul toward me. It meant that I had to be guarded in every word and action toward her, for fear of misinterpretation. And that later I would have to hurt her—for I could discover no warmer feelings toward her than admiration and friendship, search my heart as I might.

"Gretel had often spoken to me of her longing for a pet of some kind. I sent to Paris for a Persian kitten, and while her father was ill, and before she had permitted me to read her feelings so plainly, this little creature arrived and I had the pleasure of presenting it to her. The trouble I had taken to give her pleasure must have been the opening wedge in persuading her that I was more interested than I had felt wise to express. She must, in fact, have taken my gift as a delicate indication from me of a warmer feeling, for it was immediately after this that she began to treat me more as a favored lover than a friend on an intimate but impersonal footing.

"While the professor lay on his deathbed, Gretel permitted him to understand that she would not be left unprotected. I felt myself trapped. But I could not find it in my heart to deny the dying man this consolation, when with a smile of contentment on his haggard countenance he joined our hands and blessed us. In that moment Gretel lifted her face to mine for the first kiss—and I—I gave it. Such a revulsion of feeling toward her took place within me at the intimate contact that physical sickness gripped me; I felt nauseated, and was horrified that the kiss of a lovely and loving girl should affect me in such a manner. Little did I dream then why my soul, clean and uncontaminated by wilful evil, shrank from that caress.

"Into my sick ears she murmured her love. 'I would sell my very soul for your sake, Dale,' she whispered. Significant words, which at the time I hardly heeded. It was later that I was to realize what unutterably hideous things lay behind them.

"Now came the thing which has given Gretel her hold on me, a hold more powerful to bind me than steel chains could be. The deceased professor lay in his casket, surrounded by flowers, on the morning of the funeral. I was working in the laboratory on certain experiments which could not be held up, when Gretel, with white face and staring blue eyes, burst into the room. The little Persian cat had gotten into the parlor, and Gretel—knowing well what might happen—had not dared to go in after it herself.

" 'You gave it to me. The responsibility is yours, Dale. I dare not,' she said with trembling lips. Momentarily horrified though I was— for my occult studies had prepared me for such contingencies—my modern, common-sense mentality could not credit that possibility. I laughed. God help me, I laughed! Pushing her to one side gently, I went down into the parlor.

"The kitten was sunning itself at one window where the shade was up a trifle, letting in a broad beam of sunshine. Apart from that, the great apartment was in gloom, which seemed to center about the casket standing in the middle of the room, covered by flowers which shed a heavy perfume that was almost sickeningly sweet. I went toward the kitten, calling to it coaxingly. The little thing rose, arching its back and waving its plumy tail, but it would not permit my approach. When I made a quick dash forward to put my hands upon it, the small creature slithered easily away from under my clumsy fingers and bounded across the room, springing with lithe grace directly across the open casket."

The doctor's accents as he spoke these last words bore a tragic significance.

"A woman's scream rang out. Gretel, who had followed me, went down in a dead faint just on the threshold. The kitten ran across her prostrate form and out into the brighter rooms of the house. I stood for a moment, overwhelmed all at once by the realization of the horror of that curse which my knowledge of the occult told me was now upon that unfortunate house. Then I told myself furiously that I was a fool and an oaf. I went to Gretel's aid, picked up her unconscious body, and closed the room door with an uncontrollable shudder."

"Frankly, Dr. Armitage, I can see nothing in this incident to have roused you to such a fever of apprehension," objected Ewan, reaching for a match, and taking out his cigarette case, which he offered and the doctor rather impatiently refused.

Dale transfixed him with a harsh look, at which the artist squirmed uneasily.

"If I were to retail to you certain symptoms of some obscure and loathsome disease, would you feel the horror and repugnance that a brother physician might, who understood every reference and its inevitable conclusion?" asked the doctor pointedly.

Ewan's shoulders shrugged, but he continued to maintain his loftily scornful air.

"I think I remember something like that," Bessie contributed, thoughtfully. "A cat's jumping over a corpse."

The doctor nodded.

"Ancient superstitions state that this makes a vampire of the unhappy dead," he explained.

Ewan threw up both hands in a gesture of polite resignation.

"So you're going to carry us into the realms of superstition!" said he, with a light laugh. "Bessie, don't take the doctor too seriously. He's amusing himself at our expense."

"Hear me out, Gillespie. Then perhaps even you may admit that I am not amusing myself at your expense," said the doctor sternly. "That evening, after the funeral services, I made preparations for an all-night vigil with the professor's body, which was not to be put into the receiving vault until the next day. Gretel shut herself into her room, leaving everything to me. I had been busy all that afternoon and early evening, with wax and certain aromatic herbs, dipping candles with which I purposed to light and fumigate that funeral chamber. I had been unable to procure wild roses, for it was wintertime and none were in blossom, naturally. Neither could I get garlic, although I sent a maid to scour the city markets. I had been obliged to resort to whatever methods lay within my immediate power to prepare. Of the efficiency of these I was not myself persuaded."

"It was with mixed feelings of incredulity, apprehension, and intense curiosity that I closed the door of that chamber of the dead behind me, when darkness had settled down upon the city, and made ready for my long, lonely watch. A spirit lamp with coffee was ready, in case I felt drowsy, for it was all-important that my mind should be kept at its highest power, in case of some dread need that would call for all I could give of alertness. I lighted the sweet-smelling candles I had prepared, and welcomed with inward satisfaction the changing atmosphere of the room, which—until they began burning dimly, sending out their medicated, fragrant aroma—had smelled horridly of the presence of death and decay."

"Ugh!" Ewan shuddered uncontrollably. A look of involuntary satisfaction flitted across the doctor's dark face, as if he were pleased with the effect of his words upon the other man's sensibilities.

"Nothing happened until almost 3 o'clock in the morning," he went on, after a momentary pause. "It was then that I became suddenly aware that the atmosphere of the room was altering subtly; charging, as it were, with something potently malevolent in its tendencies toward me, toward that dead lying there so silent and white, and—stranger yet—toward Gretel Himmbeeren, who must have been wakeful and terrified at that crucial moment in her own room, where she had chosen to lock herself in. My aromatic candles were guttering in their sockets.

"There was a pulsing (regular and monotonous like the dizzy drumming of trance just before or after taking chloroform) in the etheric particles of the atmosphere surrounding me, that brought about a heaviness of my mental faculties, which I realized must now be awakened to a more than usually acute alertness, or I, and Gretel, and that dead, too, would become the playthings of forces of Evil, the naming of which is only too often to bring them about one," darkly.

"The wind is rising," murmured Bessie, hazel eyes all at once wide and staring like a sleep-walker's. "I can hear it coming over the tree-tops. It is whispering in the branches—getting louder and louder—and wilder. It is roaring among the forest giants, and they must be bending before it like grass under the autumn winds. Oh, Dale, look! Look at that window!"

The girl had risen from her seat and was pointing with stiff forefinger across at the window of Ewan's room. The artist turned in a flash, as did the other man.

"It was Gretel!" declared Bessie in agitation and alarm. "I saw her plainly. She stood looking at us, and laughing. Dale, she isn't dead. She must be alive yet. Oh, stop her before she can harm herself!"

The brave girl dashed to the cabin door, followed by the two men. Accompanied by the doctor, she ran around one side of the cabin, Ewan going in the opposite direction. But when they met, none of them had seen Gretel, although the doctor found footprints under Ewan's window, with deeply indented heel-prints, and Bessie's shoes were wide-heeled, not narrow and French-heeled.

"I saw her," insisted Bessie, much disturbed. "She looked at me so furiously that it terrified me. She must be hiding near us now, behind some bush or tree. Gretel!" she called, impulsively.

For a moment the startled three thought they heard a mocking laugh from the thick woods. The doctor's face was pallid, for it was impossible to locate the sound. His dark eyes were deep hollows of misery in his white countenance.

"She has managed to elude us this time," he admitted, his keen gaze seeking the forest vistas this way and that for the flash of color that would have been Gretel's sport dress. "And it must be that she is alive. That is why you heard the wind, Bessie. She would hardly be able to get across the stream without calling to her aid those Dark Powers that so recently made a frozen pathway for her over the running water. And now again," he broke off, with a gesture toward the stream, "she has come to this side of the brook."

His eyes lifted to the treetops, but they were motionless in the fresh morning air.

"I can hear the wind," persisted Bessie, puzzled, after being persuaded by her own eyes that the branches of the forest giants were still, although that ominous roaring continued loudly.

"There is mischief afoot," admitted the doctor, unwillingly. "I myself do not know in what direction Gretel may be able to turn her evil gifts. Shall we go inside again? I must complete my story before other interruptions occur, for both of you must be able to see Today in the light of Yesterday, so that you can understand better what lies before us in Tomorrow," bitterly.

The trio went inside and seated themselves about the table as before. But at the doctor's suggestion, Bessie pulled down the burlap she had tacked up over Ewan's window, but that he had drawn aside that morning when he rose.

"I believe I was telling you," the doctor began again, "that I felt a thickening, a turbidity, of the atmosphere in that death chamber, about 3 o'clock in the morning. I hastily lighted the spirit lamp—it burned with an unearthly blue flame that struck me unpleasantly at the moment, although that was its usual color—and put over it the saucepan with coffee. Then I advanced toward the casket to observe if any changes had taken place in that dead which lay so silently there.

"I turned my electric flash upon that dead face, and staggered back as if struck by a furious hand. For the dead eyes were open, observing me with a malicious intentness and a measured calculation that sent sickly shudderings down my spinal column!"

"Cataleptic trance!" jerked out Ewan distastefully. "Why try to create this ghostly atmosphere, Dr. Armitage, when the condition of that supposedly dead man was a more or less ordinary one, well known to science?"

"It was not a cataleptic trance," retorted the doctor with heat. "Will you be courteous enough to hear me out, Gillespie?"

The artist drew down the corners of his mouth but said nothing, and the physician, after a slight pause, went on.

Chapter 13
Lips of the Dead

"**I** could not, at the first horrid shock, credit the witness of my own senses, so I collected myself, breathing thickly in that turgid atmosphere that seemed swollen now with crowding heaviness that made it difficult to draw a free breath, loaded as the air was with the odor from the candles, and that strange smell of death that had now returned more strongly than ever. I turned the flash lamp full upon the professor's dead face and leaned over steadily to apprize myself of whatever the situation might be. I told myself that I had been mistaken, for the waxen eyelids were closed with the immobility of death over the once kindly eyes. Then—

"The yellowing lids quivered. They began to move upward, to fold back with a horrid, purposeful steadiness. The white eyeballs were soon showing about those gleaming, glassy eyes, as they rolled upward slowly, horribly, to meet my frozen, shrinking gaze. Professor Himmbeeren had become that unutterably awful Thing to which he had been condemned by his own reckless meddling with the Forces of Evil before he knew how to protect himself; condemned because that lack of spiritual armor had made him all too susceptible to the occult line of influence traced across his quiescent body when the Persian kitten, plaything and instrument of relentless Fate, leaped over his dead form.

"As the awful import of all this came home to my sick soul, I tore my almost paralyzed gaze from that of the now grinning Thing in the casket, and brought all my mental faculties to a point, to stop at once the ghastly sequence of events that now seemed shaping. Strange as it may seem to you, I—theoretically believing in the possibility of the thing that had now taken place before me—had been unable to credit its practical possibility. So have many human souls been lost, that have walked the forbidden paths, believing, they did not prepare for what their studies must have told them were possible contingencies.

"I had remained on guard that night to see that the dead man's body remained undisturbed, but the very reason of my presence in that room had not penetrated sufficiently into my mind for me to have provided myself with the means of putting a stop to any such occult manifestations of evil as had now become evident. I needed garlic, cloves. I should have been prepared with a sharpened stake, a keen-edged surgical knife, a wooden mallet. Even the simple precaution of a crucifix on the dead lips I had neglected. Of these essentials I had quite nothing. And that was not the moment to seek them. I stood there helpless, unable to send into the peace of real death that Thing that now stirred softly, horridly, in the casket, as it took completer command of its new domicile and future instrument, the dead man's body.

"I stood there in dire stress, neither daring to retreat and leave the Thing to its own ghastly devices while I hunted for what I had need, nor daring approach it again, for I was only a weak man, and it was—but it is better not to breathe that terrible name, for the very reverberations of those sounds will set the delicate ether about us to quivering and quaking, and upon those waves of vibration it can the better reach us now," shuddered the doctor.

Ewan sucked in his breath with a gasping sound.

"As a teller of ghost stories, Armitage," said he disgustedly, "you are certainly without peer. I am absolutely scared into shivers. All of which may be highly gratifying to you, but I resent having my sister terrified into convulsions by this yam you insist upon getting off your chest."

"Shall I stop, Bessie? Is it too much for you?"

Bessie shook her head emphatically.

"No, Dale. If Ewan doesn't care to listen, he can leave us. I intend to hear all you feel you can tell," she declared.

Ewan grunted in disgust but showed no signs of leaving them. The doctor waited for a moment, then picked up the thread of his story once more.

"While I stood there, listening with the utmost loathing to the soft stirrings in the coffin, and trying to collect my scattered wits and overcome my instinctive hatred and disgust as well, I must confess, as my fear and dread, the parlor door sprang open and a white-robed apparition came swiftly over the threshold as if drawn by some power other than that of its own volition. I cried out sharply.

"And then I saw that it was Gretel who advanced toward me like a woman in a trance, her blue eyes alight with an ecstasy of horror and loathing, mingled with exultation that was impossible for me to understand at the time. She swept toward me, then veered sharply to one side until she had reached the casket. She began to bend over it, in that unearthly silence and tenseness, broken only by the stirrings from within the coffin.

"And as she bent forward, that which had been gathering its horrid forces together in the dead man's body lifted the rigid form until the ghoulish and distorted face was staring at me over the edge of the coffin! My God, my God, I can see it now!"

The doctor broke off with a gasping for breath, as if his throat muscles were constricted and he fighting for air.

"Dale! Poor Dale!"

"My dear, forgive my weakness." He mastered himself by a supreme effort. "Speaking of that unutterably fulsome and nauseous Thing that rose into sight beyond Gretel's stooping figure brought back to me all the horror of that awful night!"

"Go on!" It was Ewan's sharp voice that brought the doctor back to the present. "Get on with this yarn, for heaven's sake. I'm glad for my sister's sake that it's daylight now, and not night."

"As that malignant Thing lifted the dead body by imperceptible but steady force into a sitting posture, Gretel leaned more and more, until she was lying supine across the coffin, her flaxen hair tumbling in abandon among the fading flowers of the funeral wreaths with their sickeningly heavy odors. There she lay, twisted so that her head tilted backward, her white throat exposed in a long, lovely line, upon which the glaring, hellblasting eyes of that abhorrent Monstrosity from the Pit were now fixed with avid, unslaked cupidity.

"The Thing was so sure of itself and its potent influence over both of us, that it disdained to pay me more than that first scornful, slighting attention, and centered itself, with gaping, slobbering lips, in all the potentiality of its vile, obscene being, upon that feast which awaited its ghoulish pleasure.

"I stood there like a bit of sculptured marble, incapable of moving hand or foot; horrified into a muscular paralysis which made quite impossible the coordination of my will and my limbs. And so it came to pass that I was the unwilling, the nauseated, the wretched witness of Gretel Himmbeeren's undoing. Chained to the spot by my miserably unresponding body, I was obliged to see those gloating eyes roll over the lovely face and bosom and rest with hungry, urgent triumph upon the white neck.

"I had to see, while my soul sickened within to the point of physical nausea, the drooling mouth approaching the helpless girl's flesh, to desecrate it so horribly. My quivering nerves rebelled, but I could not even enjoy the respite that might have been mine could I have closed my eyes, so rigid had my entire body become.

"I saw the withdrawal of those wet lips from the teeth that had grown like needles, so pointed sharp did they glisten. I saw the mumbling of the girl's white skin between them, with its sickening mockery of a lover's caress. Until all at once—as if the Thing could no longer endure the delicious agony of anticipation—the teeth met, and her body, held now by two long, rigid arms, shook convulsively as the unspeakable Horror sucked rapaciously at her life's blood.

"God! God!"

"And you stood there, you miserable coward!" snapped out the artist, all at once touched to the verge of credulity by the doctor's sincere accents and his obvious suffering. "And let that poor, lovely girl be raped of her life-blood! Jove, but you are a poor apology for a man!"

Bessie had not moved. Horrified at this climax to the doctor's tragic story, she sat as if frozen, tears dimming her hazel eyes and creeping down her pale cheeks as she suffered vicariously with him.

"I do not blame you for your scorn," said the doctor sadly. "Only too many times since that fatal night have I told myself the same. Yet—the fact remains—I was as helpless that moment as if I had been chained with weighted gyves on every limb. I am not to be blamed if I had my muscles contract and they refused obedience. Yet—I forgive you for your harsh words, because I can readily understand how difficult it is to realize what my situation was.

"Well—I was fettered by inhibitions too powerful for my weak will to overcome. It seemed to me that centuries passed before the Thing removed its gaping, flabby mouth, drooling now with hot crimson, from Gretel's tender flesh. It let her body drop callously, for it was surfeited with its long drink. It rolled those gleaming, hellish orbs upon me as I stood paralyzed. Something like a scornful smile twisted the distorted features and left that wry expression permanently as the Thing stared at me.

"I could bear no more. My nerves had been drained of all surplus resources, as had Gretel's veins been drained of much blood. When the ghoulish Thing slid supinely back into the casket with the dithering movement and whishing sound of a serpent, my vocal chords all at once found freedom from tension, and I uttered a loud shriek, and then another, and fell forward upon my face, unconscious.

"The servants rushed in and found us there: Gretel upon the floor, paler than the dead lying in the casket with wry, twisted face; I on the other side of the coffin, in the first delirium of what became a raging brain fever—"

"Which explains, without further words, your whole obsession," interrupted the artist, with a nervous, half-angry look at his sister, upon whose pallid face tears were still wet. "For heaven's sake, cut out this ghastly tale, Armitage. It's unnecessary. The whole business was only too obviously a hallucination, due to approaching illness."

Dr. Armitage shook his head slowly, mournfully.

"No, Gillespie. It was the cause, not the result," he insisted, firm lips in a determined line. "And now I must insist upon your listening to all the story, since you have heard so much and are yet unconvinced. If Gretel were here, in her better mood, she would verify and confirm all that I have told, and—and have yet to tell."

Ewan rose jerkily from his chair.

"Well, I suppose Bessie will insist upon having it all," said he, disgustedly. "As for me, I've heard enough. Your wife isn't here, you see, to verify your hallucinations. And I, for one, don't intend to listen to any such ghoulish yarns in her absence. I'm sure she would agree with me that you'd had an hallucination, due to approaching illness."

He went out of the living room into his own room, deliberately pulling the door closed.

Bessie stretched her hands across the table.

"Go on. Dale. Oh, my poor dear, how you must have suffered! And poor Gretel! I cannot blame her, now that I know—"

"Wait, Bessie. Do not pity her too much," warned the doctor. "Wait until you have heard all."

With fresh anticipation of new horrors yet to come, Bessie sat up straighter, again resting her round chin in her palms as she listened intently.

"I knew nothing of what happened, until I came out of my stupor and delirium, later. I had a severe siege of it, naturally. And during my illness I had no more devoted nurse than Gretel, who spent every moment at my bedside as soon as she was physically able. This made it more difficult for me to tell her what I felt I must in honor; that while I admired and esteemed and—now—pitied her, I did not care for her as a man must care for the woman he wishes to make his wife."

Bessie's face grew warmer under the doctor's look.

"And I found it impossible, finally, to tell her this," confessed Dr. Armitage reluctantly. "The fact that I had given her the Persian kitten; that it had been I who had inadvertently sent it leaping across her father's coffin; that I had, moreover, remained a witness, although unwilling, of her initiation into vampirism; all these things were against me. She managed to make me feel that I owed her everything a man could possibly owe a loving woman. I was helpless; chained by my conviction that no matter how innocent I was, yet something of blame was mine for what had happened. By the fetters my conscience bound about me, Gretel drew me on, and a day came when we were pronounced man and wife."

"Perhaps—if you had loved her—?"

"Bessie, that might have made me her weak victim, later. I must get on with this . . . On our wedding night I felt that I had made what reparation I could, by giving her my name, the promise of my constant protection. I could go no farther. I went into the room where she awaited me, lovely in gleaming white satin, her flaxen hair undulating loosely about her shoulders, and told her clumsily that while I would devote every fiber of my being to restoring her to the full freedom of a clean soul, I could not give her the physical return which she certainly must feel her own passion merited. In plain words, I would protect her and keep her from harming others, for her own sake, but I could never be a husband to her.

"Good God, what a living fury sprang into unsuspected existence at my ultimatum! At first she clung to me, curling her body about me, writhing like a serpent into my arms, her fingers in my hair and on my face. When she found me unstirred, she changed her tactics, and reproached me with having wilfully won her heart only to crush her. When that again failed to move me, she screamed out her innermost soul, laid bare her deepest secrets before my appalled eyes!

"Then I learned that she, in her passion for evil, had mastered languages only that she might delve into forbidden tomes of base knowledge. Too light-natured to undertake the study of the deeper undertones of occultism, she let her feet stray into dubious paths. She found a road that took her by imperceptible degrees down to a door that opened into Hell," said the doctor, his voice lowering as if he feared to be overheard.

"Dale, how dreadful! Oh, the poor thing!"

"Perhaps I am hard toward her, Bessie, because I know how evil she is, and how she has wilfully fostered the growth of darkness in her own soul, and bidden welcome to whatever spirit approached her, provided it catered to her own ends.

"Down that path Gretel had walked with wilful eyes wide open, for she discovered that it is easier to slip down than to climb, and she had not the perseverance and courage for the upward struggle. She had also opened her soul to the influence of a certain evil entity—I must not say that name aloud—a certain—suffice it to say that she became animated at times by that Power to which she had willingly bowed her proud head, and it was at the intimation of that Power that she had made me understand that she wanted the kitten, and that same awful power had promised me to her if she would put the little thing into the funeral chamber, thus opening the way for It to utilize her own father's dead body. Incredible? Not to the evil thing that Gretel had become.

"In her fury of disappointment, she disclosed all this to me, so filling me with horror that the mere thought of her kiss was sufficient to fill me with sick nausea. She was the more bitter, because that Power to which she had given herself had taken toll of her, as I have told you, at the very first opportunity, planning no doubt to take me, through her, later. Now she was marked by her terrible and ruthless master, and would remain a living fountain of blood for his unslaking thirst, and at her death she could not die, but would join the sad ranks of those whom we call vampires; forced to prey upon her nearest and dearest to keep alive the spirit of evil that would occupy her helpless body.

"Her feeling of rage against what she now termed her useless sacrifice almost consumed her. She called down against that dread Power all the evil of which her strange knowledge had given her cognizance. She invoked against me all the pride of her proud nature; all the strength of her physical passion; all the cunning in her twisted brain that might serve to swerve my standards of right and wrong and deliver me into her hands.

"In vain. I had seen all only too clearly. There is in my soul the upward striving for the triumph of Light which forbids, in every fiber of my being, any compromise with the powers of Darkness. Once convinced of my determination, Gretel became suddenly meek, but not before she had warned me in her fury that she would yet make me her very own, in a far different sense from what she had expected when she believed herself loved by me. And she warned me that she would, to keep herself strongly alive for my future torment, and to prepare her own body against other visits from that dread and greedy-lipped master of hers, take toll of other human beings when and where she could.

"After that there was but one thing to do, and I did it. I kept constant watch over her. At night I arranged so that she should never be beyond surveillance. Yet she has evaded me, as that newspaper clipping told you. To save that poor child from a wretched fate, I was obliged to perform the bizarre but merciful acts that gave the poor thing's soul peace.

"In her better moments Gretel agreed to my precautions, but she would undo them by telling acquaintances that I was brutal and jealous, until I often found my hands tied by her evil cunning. Your brother, for example, considers her a persecuted angel," he remarked abruptly.

"And now, Bessie, we are almost at the end of the story. We came out here, after I found that she had impregnated that poor child, with the intention of working the thing out by ourselves, away from other people. I knew that this might conceivably end by my becoming her victim, but I had taken precautions to leave a will which provided for such a contingency. I refer, Bessie, to the cleanly practice of cremation, which would put an end, if universally practiced, to very nearly all the hauntings and the cases of vampirism and lycanthropy which arise from time to time.

"We had hardly been here a month, before you and your brother came. Gretel was aflame with obscene thirst; it had been some time since she had tasted blood. When you told me you intended to remain near us all summer, an intolerable psychic apprehension, amounting to actual pain, arose within me. I struck at the wooden railing with my fist, bruising it in the hope of inducing a physical pain that would deaden my intuitional alarm. To think of you, so unsuspecting, waiting for her to pounce upon you—!

"That night I told her calmly that I would kill her with my own hands, rather than let her continue her evil courses. She laughed at me. She reminded me that she would be freer dead than living. Then I foolishly told her that I had prepared to lay that evil spirit and free her soul from the curse she had herself brought upon it.

"And then she was afraid, and became crafty. And now—my God, I have let her escape me! She will be able to take flight as she has so often threatened, and she will hide her body, and she will roam free over the face of the earth. And your poor brother, my Bessie, has been infected, and she can call him to her at will!"

Chapter 14
The Return of the Undead

As if conjured by the mention of himself, Ewan opened his door wide and stood there for a moment looking out upon the two. A secret smile of superiority curled his lips. He was carrying a knapsack which bulged as if it were heavily stuffed.

"It's 10 o'clock," said he abruptly. "I can't afford to waste this glorious summer morning, listening to ghost stories. I'm on my way upstream a bit, Bessie. I may not be back for lunch, but I've taken some chocolate, so I shan't starve. You coming my way?" he added suddenly, pointedly addressing the doctor.

Dale rose with a slight contraction of his forehead. "I still have something to talk over with your sister, Gillespie," said he with too much seriousness for Ewan to take offense. "And then I must try to find Gretel, dead or alive."

Ewan hesitated, then burst out with obvious reluctance. "She isn't dead, Armitage. I've seen her. I know her plans and I approve them. She would be foolish indeed to submit herself to you, to be put under lock and key like a dangerous lunatic. She is alive and well, and," he finished hastily as the doctor sprang to his feet and confronted him with agitation, "and you won't find her."

"You have seen her! When? Where? Thank God she still lives! That means there is hope for you, yet!"

Ewan stepped back a few paces toward the outer door of the cabin, his eyes on the doctor.

"I don't suppose it will do any harm to tell you," he argued as if with himself.

"Where did you see Gretel?" demanded the doctor sternly. "Answer at once!"

"Put it that way, and see what you'll get," retorted the artist truculently.

"Ewan—please!"

Ewan's head jerked angrily. "Well, if I must, Bessie—a few minutes ago, I saw her. She came to my window and I climbed out, and we talked. She has no intention of putting herself back into your hands, Armitage. In my opinion she would be quite unjustified in doing so, after the insane way you've been acting and talking."

"Ewan!"

"Well, Bessie, if you'd listen to me, you'd send this man packing. That poor girl has been bulldozed by him for a long time, but she has rebelled at last. I advised her to go to a—to a kind of cave I found in the woods the other day. I do not advise you, Armitage, to attempt finding that cave, for your wife has my pistol, which I gave her at her own request to defend herself in case of need, and I have a strong feeling that she will shoot anybody who intrudes upon her to deprive her of her freedom," Ewan declared.

"He has given her the means of carrying out her threat!" said the doctor to Bessie. "I must find her if I can, before it is too late . . . Perhaps I can persuade her to hark to the dictates of a conscience that I cannot believe is entirely dead within her. Keep the cabin door closed, Bessie. And put that branch of wild rose over the lintel. You must understand very clearly by now what her entrance here would mean to you."

Seeing that the doctor was about to leave, Ewan turned and went briskly across the clearing. The other two watched him out of sight.

"Couldn't you have given that dead professor peace, Dale? Wouldn't that have healed Gretel?" asked Bessie, then.

"She refused me access to her father's tomb. And as I saw her inclined more and more to fall within that circle of evil influence, I brought her here, or she would have been drained by her Master of the last drop of blood. But some day I must return to Munich and somehow manage to gain access to the professor's tomb, and—do that which will give him peace."

Bessie shuddered.

"It is horrible, Dale."

"Yes, brown Bessie, it is horrible. But now I must look for Gretel or she will manage to lure your brother to his doom. Pray that he may return to you in safety tonight," he added darkly.

"Must I remain alone, Dale?"

"I shall come back at nightfall and stay until dawn," the doctor reassured her comfortingly. "I cannot risk your being alone here, with Gretel unleashed."

Even with that promise to depend upon, Bessie did not spend a very happy day. She remained within doors, barring the way that might otherwise give entree to Gretel. When afternoon shadows began to stretch long lines across the clearing, she watched more and more anxiously for her brother. Just before dark he came out of the wood. Without paying any attention to her, he walked purposefully into the inner room and began tearing down the wild rose sprays from window and door.

"Ewan, what are you doing?" his sister called in sharp anxiety.

"I'm not going to have these ridiculous things here, Bessie," said he resentfully. "Lot of superstitious rubbish that fellow's been stuffing you with. What earthly good are these dried things, I ask you? Use your head, sis. He can't put it over on me, and if you weren't so credulous, you'd see how silly his story is, too. Tonight you will find that nothing extraordinary will happen, except that poor Gretel will have a chance for a good night's sleep in peace and safety."

"Gretel? Not here?" ejaculated the girl, her face pallid, her eyes staring at him wildly.

"Here," he responded tersely. "Do you suppose I'd let her spend the night out in the woods? I'll sleep out here in a bunk, and she shall have my room. Tomorrow I'll take her down to Amity Dam, and then—" but his look grew slyly secretive.

"And then—!" prompted Bessie, apprehensively.

"You'd like to know, wouldn't you, Bessie? So you could notify that fellow? Well, sis, you're not going to find out. What have you got for supper? I left Gretel my flashlight, so that she could find her way through the woods, and she'll be hungry."

"Hungry?" gasped Bessie, shrinking. "Ewan, I can't have that girl in here. I just can't."

"Don't be a goose, sis. And when she comes, be decent to her. She's had a time with that fellow, Bessie, and you could see with half an eye that he's off his bat, only you're so hypnotized by his big black eyes and his Vandyke beard," disgustedly, "that you really think this silly rot he's stuffed you with is true."

Ewan finished tearing down the wild rose sprays, and was opening the cabin door to put them out when Bessie stopped him.

"Leave them on the floor in the corner, Ewan," she said, as casually as she could. "I'll put them out later. Or I could use them for light kindling."

Ewan dropped them indifferently.

"As long as they're not draped about the house, I don't care," he said.

In a few minutes Ewan was eating hungrily, his back to the door, for Bessie had cunningly placed his chair so that he could not look from the window across the clearing.

"Now I'll put these things out," said she aloud, and picked up the dried branches.

"That's the girl," applauded her brother.

Bessie hastily tiptoed to the small room, and with trembling fingers hung what branches she could about the window and over the lintel of the inner door. Then she slipped out of the cabin, one remaining spray of withered wild rose still in her shaking hands.

Out of the forest depths twinkled the ray of an electric flash. Now and then, as the holder advanced, it turned upon his face, as if to notify and reassure any watcher in the cabin.

"Dale! It is you! Thank God!"

Bessie almost fell into the doctor's astonished arms, as he came out into the clearing.

"What has happened?"

She told him quickly, in broken phrases.

"He has been with her today, and she is now preparing for her entry tonight," declared the doctor tensely. "It is her influence that made him tear down the rose sprays. Bessie, she must not be allowed to enter! It might mean your brother's death—or yours, brown girl."

Bessie held out the withered spray of wild rose.

"I can put this over the cabin door. I've put the others back into Ewan's room, but he'll be furious when he sees them. If he takes them down, I won't remain in the cabin. I'd rather drown myself than face Gretel again," she said passionately.

The doctor cut off the light from his electric flash.

"I'll watch here for Gretel. I will intercept her. There is one last resort for tonight—until I can provide myself with the right articles to put a stop to her wickedness. I pray God I may not have to use that last resort, though, for the thought of it sickens me."

"What is that, Dale?"

He stared at her in the dusk.

"If I am unable to persuade her in any other way, I shall let her have her will of me," he said.

"Dale! Dale! Not that! I refuse to be saved by such a sacrifice. But—what if Ewan pulls down the sprays?"

The doctor thought a moment. He drew a small case of vials from his pocket, turning the flash upon it. He selected a bottle, tipped a couple of tablets onto his palm and gave them to the girl.

"Put these into his food," he ordered. "He'll probably go into a doze, and he shouldn't wake until morning. Before he gets fully asleep, get him into his room and shut him in with the wild rose sprays."

Urged by the doctor's gentle hand at her elbow, Bessie went back to the cabin with the tablets.

"Go with God, my brown maid," he whispered, and at the door his lips brushed her cheek. "I shall watch over you tonight, my dear one."

Bessie closed the door loudly. Ewan turned at the sound.

"Glad you got rid of that rubbish, sis," said he. "Tea ready? I'll pour myself a cupful."

Almost in a panic, she pulled the cup from his hand.

"Sit down, Ewan, do. I'll pour it for you. You're—you're tired, being out in the woods all day."

Her back turned, she slipped the tablets into the steaming amber beverage and then watched them impatiently as they dissolved with exasperating slowness. When the last drop in the cup had gone down Ewan's throat she felt more relaxed, especially as she noticed in a few minutes that his eyelids were dropping drowsily.

"I'll stay out here, sis. Fix up my room for Gretel, will you?" he murmured heavily.

Bessie guided his feet into his own room, glad that he was so sleepy by now that he did not realize where he was going. Thankfulness in her heart, she saw him slip down and begin breathing heavily. She saw to it that the burlap was pulled well across the window, and that the rose sprays were in place about it, as well as secure over the lintel. Then she shut the door with the feeling that he, at least, was safe for the time being.

She had not yet barred the outer door, nor had she had time, with Ewan watching her, to put that other rose spray over the lintel. Now she turned to take this last precaution. And as she turned, she heard a soft rustling at the door, such as a serpent makes among dead autumn leaves, and the latch lifted with menacing slowness that froze her with alarm where she stood.

The door opened. Bessie retreated against the inner door, her heart beating painfully against her side. The door swung wide. There was the whisking of garments, and Gretel glided in, pushed the door to, and turned to Bessie, her sharp white teeth glistening in the lamplight.

"How disappointed you must have felt, sweetheart, that we were interrupted last night! Was it for that you left the latch up for me? Well, I am here, Bessie. And tonight there shall be no interruptions. I left Dale far out in the woods," she laughed shrilly. "I led him a merry chase. He is upstream now, running about with his electric flashlight and calling me, and threatening me with dire things if I don't answer!"

She threw back her head, until the flaxen locks tumbled about her shoulders, so white and smooth in the friendly light of the kerosene lamp. She laughed softly, triumphantly, cunningly. Then, her red tongue lapping delicately at her vivid lips, she turned the full, hypnotic gaze of her luridly blazing eyes upon the shrinking girl, with such confidence in her power to bend her to her will that Bessie quaked inwardly, although she met the look bravely, sheer desperation bracing her into outward composure.

"You thought Dale would be watching over you, didn't you, Bessie, my dear?" softly asked the doctor's wife, her shoulders shaking with malicious merriment. "Well, I saw to it that he'd be far enough away tonight. There'll be plenty of time for me—for us, Bessie—before he comes. As for your brother, when I'm ready for him I'll call him, but just now I'm going to punish Dale through you.

"I shall take all you have to give me tonight. I'm through with being modest in my demands," she leered. "I'm thirsty, Bessie. And when you're mine, you shall bring Dale to me, yourself. Ah, that will be a sweet revenge! And you shall be as I am now," and she lifted one hand to push aside the tumbling flaxen locks from her left temple. "Today I put a bullet through my head with your brother's revolver. That has freed me forever from Dale's idiotic assumption of authority. That is, unless he finds my body, and I've taken precious good care that he shan't," she added, viciously.

Bessie's cold lips stammered:

"But you're—not—dead?"

Gretel laughed shrilly.

"Poor Bessie! You can't understand it, can you? Come to me and judge for yourself," she invited. "Feel the chill of my hand—and the death-sweat on my brow—and put your finger, if you will, into this bullet wound—"

Horror overcame Bessie.

"Dale! Help! Dale!" she found herself screaming wildly.

Scornful amusement played over Gretel's pallid, waxen face.

"He cannot come, Bessie. Not now. He is too far away. And when he comes, you will be very white, Bessie, and I shall be rosy-red with color from the warm blood you are going to give me now." She laughed again.

Bessie's wide eyes stared at the doctor's wife fixedly, incredulously. She was pressing her cold hands against her trembling mouth. She was telling herself that she must not—must not—wake Ewan.

"But how silly we are, talking away precious, delicious moments," whispered Gretel, advancing sinuously, the red lights in her eyes blazing with hypnotic power upon Bessie, who shrank back in spite of herself against that inner door.

"You are going to—to kill me—tonight?" she managed to gasp through dry, working lips.

Gretel stopped short for a moment. Sly cunning wrote her thoughts across her cold face.

"No, sweetheart, after all I won't—not tonight. Don't be afraid. I shall only take enough to warm me a little and to assuage my thirst—you are so full of rich, red blood, Bessie, that it does my heart good to look at you," she enthused mockingly. "Come to me, Bessie. Come! You don't want to hear me call your brother?" she insinuated, craftily, and smiled at the quick start that the other girl gave at her words.

"Oh no—not Ewan!"

"Then come to me of your own free will," coaxed Gretel. "It won't hurt, I promise. Only for a tiny moment. You cannot imagine how delicious it is to feel my lips against your throat, brown girl—once my sharp teeth have met in your tender flesh. There is even an ecstasy in being absorbed into another's being, as I draw your life out through your pierced vein. I know—I know! It will be wonderful—I promise you.

"Come! I shall kiss you hotly, ardently, as no lover has ever kissed you, sweetheart. Come to me! Of your own free will!"

As she spoke, Gretel came closer, sliding silently, sinuously, until her hands touched Bessie's, drawing the other girl's fingers down from the terror-glazed eyes. The icy thrill of those terrible fingers froze Bessie, so that she stood, unable to move.

"I told you I would return to you in anger, but I hadn't the heart, sweet," murmured the doctor's wife sibilantly. "You are so rosy and round, Bessie, that I long to have you offer yourself instead of being obliged to. Be still, foolish girl! I am stronger than you. It is futile to struggle against the Undead. And do not shrink.

"In a moment I shall kiss you, and then you will thrill as you never dreamed you could. My poor pale cheeks will grow pink with your warm blood, Bessie, and I shall love you because of the life you are giving me. And I shall come to you again soon—very soon—so that you can yield me the last drop in your veins, and then—and then—I'll show you how to win Dale to us, Bessie!"

The hateful, sinuous arms held Bessie tight, clipped her against the algid chill of Gretel's bosom. The red lips drew back against the gums, and the sharp, glistening white teeth were disclosed.

"Do not struggle so, Bessie! Tip your head back—so. Ah!"

Bessie felt herself swooning.

"This time," was her last conscious thought, "I am lost indeed!"

Chapter 15
Gretel Drives a Bargain

The cabin door flew open. Into the room, like an avenging fury, strode Dale Armitage, dark eyes flashing, face working with anxiety.

"Put that girl down!" he shouted, as he crossed the threshold and sprang toward the two women.

He put his arms across Gretel's shoulders, loosening her hold and jerking her brutally awry from the fainting girl, who staggered back against Ewan's door.

Gretel's face altered subtly from its alluring sweetness into that semblance of a thwarted fiend that was so horrible. She twisted from her husband's grasp and again flung herself upon Bessie, who had no time even to throw her hands before her throat in self-protection.

"I shall have her!" screamed Gretel shrilly. "She is mine, I tell you."

Again the doctor pulled her away, this time jerking her about until he stood between the two women; the trembling Bessie, and the palpitating, furious Undead with gnashing teeth.

"She is not yours," he retorted sternly. "And you shall never have her. Not while I live to prevent it."

"You think because you hold me here that you have won the game," replied his wife furiously. "Today I put a bullet through my head. See?" and she pulled from him, shaking her head until the wound could be plainly observed in her left temple.

"If I keep you here until daylight, Gretel," said the doctor, with repugnance, "you cannot escape me. Your body will be under my control, for you will have no chance to hide it away before sunrise. And then I shall do to it what must be done," said he, sternly.

In Gretel's drooping mien, her slyly veiled eyes, cunning concealed itself none too well. She leaned languorously toward him.

"Dale—if it is you who holds me—my only love! Keep me close to your side all night, my dear, my dearest! And then tomorrow—free me!"

The doctor's grasp relaxed, ever so slightly. In that unguarded moment she pulled away from him and stood swaying in the open doorway.

"Don't make one step toward me, Dale. One movement, and I shall be gone, and you cannot follow my flight or find where I shall hide my body before day breaks. Ahriman will sweep me away on the winds, as he has done before!"

Dale groaned: "Fool that I am!"

Softly, alluringly, Gretel laughed. With such sweetness did she hold out her white arms to him that Bessie, leaning on the table, felt that magnetic undercurrent of power thrilling in her own veins and half rose, still under the hypnotism of Gretel's influence. The doctor's wife saw this and flung back her flaxen head, laughing again that shrilly triumphant laughter that Bessie dreaded, so did it draw upon her tense nerves, titillating them beyond endurance.

"Something of a fool you are, and always have been, Dale," agreed the Undead scornfully. "And I was stupid enough to love you! Dale, I make a bargain with you. Ewan is mine; I have but to call him and he will tear down the fragile barriers you have placed between us, and come to me, to offer me the remaining drops of his blood. As for Bessie—look at her—and see if she is not already mine! Mine to call, because she has yielded in spirit to my stronger will not once, but twice."

The doctor looked and groaned again, for Bessie's soft hazel eyes had grown hard and staring, fixed upon Gretel's redly glowing orbs. Even as he watched, the girl began to move uncertainly toward the outer door where Gretel beckoned. For a moment there was tense silence; then came the sound of crackling, dried branches. The door of the inner room opened and from it were thrust the withered rose sprays Bessie had placed there to protect her brother. Ewan, somehow sensing the undercurrents of tense emotion, had wakened, and in another minute would emerge, to fall also under the terrible spell of the Undead...

Through the dulling senses of Bessie there penetrated the realization of her brother's imminent danger. Suddenly, as if in a panic, she ran straight past the horrified physician and into the outstretched arms of the smiling Gretel, who received the fainting body and lifted it tightly clutched against her breast.

"Not Ewan!" panted Bessie incoherently. "Take me—instead!"

Dale Armitage lifted both hands in resignation. He took one look toward the other room, in the doorway of which Ewan now stood like a man entranced, waiting to be called by that terrible Undead to which he had become enslaved. He gave one yearning look at the body of the girl he loved, lying laxly against Gretel's breast. Then—

"Well, do you accept the bargain?" crisply demanded his wife. "I give you both these, Dale, on one condition."

"And that—?" he whispered hoarsely, hopelessly.

"Sweet Bessie has given herself to me of her own will," proceeded Gretel calmly. "Her brother only awaits my call, to offer me what remains of his blood. And—oh, Ahriman, how I thirst!"

As if she could no longer restrain herself, she arched her neck and plunged her face downward in a long curve upon Bessie's throat.

The doctor, with an incoherent exclamation, sprang frantically forward. He pushed up that flaxen head until the blazing, hell-blasting eyes met his own desperate ones. He tugged impotently at the arms that clutched Bessie's body.

"Let her go! She is an innocent girl. I—I give in, Gretel!" he groaned in agony of spirit.

His wife let the other girl's body drop callously to the floor, as she read in Dale's eyes his surrender.

"Oh, Dale, my love! At last!" she breathed. "Ahriman did not lie to me! Through devious ways I have sought your love. Dale. I have sold my soul to gain you. And now—? You will give yourself to me freely? I may slake my thirst from your veins, until you leave your fainting body to become my eternal companion? Ahriman! Ahriman!" she shrilled in an abandonment of wild, eery triumph, waving her arms in the air as she conjured.

The rising of an icy wind came suddenly upon the little group with a tearing blast of piercing cold. Gretel pulled at the doctor's arm. He jerked away from her, as if half entranced but desperately resisting. Stiffly as an automaton, he backed away from her, picking up the limp form of Bessie and lifting it in his arms. She stared at him, suspicion darkening her waxen face.

"I must first say good-bye to Bessie," said the doctor sharply.

Gretel shrugged her shoulders carelessly.

"Do not be too long about it," she warned ominously. "My patience has been tried severely, Dale."

Bessie flung up her arms and caught the doctor about the neck, as he laid her on the cot in the living room.

"Dale, don't go! Rather let it be me!" she implored.

He shook his head emphatically. "This is my responsibility, brown girl. Tomorrow you will leave this accursed spot. If God gives me strength, I shall live tomorrow, for I do not believe she can drain all my life from me tonight," said he significantly. "Later you will return to the lodge, if you have the courage, and you will see that our bodies—"

"Oh, Dale, Dale!" she broke into soft, bitter weeping.

"—that our bodies," he went on inexorably, "are cremated on a pyre of mountain ash."

"I could not! I could not!"

"What I ask you, Bessie, is love's greatest sacrifice," he told her solemnly. "Unless you do this, I must go on into eternity—Undead— accursed."

"I promise!" she choked.

"God bless you, dear."

His cheek touched hers. Vaguely she sensed that he dared not kiss her; he had dedicated himself to Evil and would not contaminate her purity. Then he was gone. His footsteps died away in the quiet night.

The icy blast that had risen at Gretel's conjurations now began to scream and whistle about the little cabin. It tore at the door Dale had closed behind him as he went to make his sublime sacrifice.

And in his doorway Ewan stood with suddenly alert eyes, listening to his sister sobbing as if her heart would break. Across his face passing thoughts sent drifting expressions that clearly portrayed his bewilderment of mind and spirit.

Was he mad? Was Bessie mad? Or were those others—?

One dominant thought, one urging purpose, arose in his mind. He and Bessie must leave that unholy place, at the earliest opportunity.

Chapter 16
The Funeral Pyre

Early afternoon of the following day. Bessie had finished packing up her own and her brother's belongings, under Ewan's pressing orders.

"We're going down to Amity Dam this afternoon," he had said to her, finality in voice and mien. "There's too much of the outre about this whole situation. The pair of them are crazy as loons. Ought to be put away, both of them, for the safety of sane folk," he had added with what the girl recognized as resentment at the way he had been obliged to alter his set opinion of Gretel Armitage.

"Can't we wait a little longer?" the girl pleaded, longing with all her heart to get out of her brother's sight and hunt at the lodge for Dale.

"Sorry, Bessie, but it isn't a case now of what you want to do. That fellow has gotten you half scared to death with his ghastly yarns. As for me, I'm as nervous and shaky as the very dickens, and I don't intend to put in the rest of the summer in such shape. No, sis, we don't stay here. We're going, before night," he finished, with such an expression on his face that Bessie knew that he was now realizing acutely that there was something uncanny about the strange experiences that had befallen them both, little as he cared to acknowledge it.

In silence she had begun packing. The cabin was soon denuded of cooking utensils, blankets, pillows, painting paraphernalia. Already the rooms wore an air of desolation that struck painfully at Bessie's spirit.

"After we've had a bite to eat, sis, we'll get these last things into the canoe," said Ewan briskly. "And before dusk we ought to be down at the village. Going with the stream, you know, makes the trip down quite nothing."

Mechanically Bessie began to prepare that last little meal, a cold one save for the tea, since almost everything but the necessary food had been packed away in the canoe.

"Jove, sis! Be careful there! You'll scald yourself!" came Ewan's warning cry, as the girl snatched up the teakettle, then set it hastily down again, so that the boiling water slopped steaming upon the hot surface of the stove.

Bessie was not listening. She had run to the cabin door and out, and was across the clearing like a deer, to meet the man who, with dragging steps, slowly advanced toward the cabin.

"Dale!"

He held her off, unsteady hands extended against her nearer approach. His dark eyes were pools of exhaustion in a pallid, bloodless face. His lips were white, tight-drawn against his teeth, showing the bloodless gums.

"No, Bessie. Not yet," said he, each word coming with the gasping emphasis that bespoke the struggle it cost him to speak with his waning strength. "Not yet—dear."

"Oh, my dear, you are alive! Thank God! Thank God!"

"Alive?" A laugh jerked from him that was like a cry.

"You are going with us, aren't you. Dale? If you aren't, then I shall stay," said the girl firmly.

"Go!"

"I cannot," said her dry lips. "I cannot leave you. My place is at your side."

A faint smile flickered over the doctor's chalky face.

"Then—take me—with you," he whispered, and stumbled toward the cabin. "I—have performed what I had to, upon her body, this morning. But—Bessie—never ask me of last night! It must be a closed book between us, unutterably terrible—unreadable."

Incredulous joy seized upon the girl, despite his words.

"But before I go—I must await— the healing—of this." His hand went to his neck in a piteous gesture. "Because I gave myself of my own free will, I am not yet healed."

Ewan's voice sounded brusquely from the cabin.

"My neck's healed!" he cried out sharply. "Those little wounds have disappeared!"

Fixing the artist with his hollow eyes, the doctor said, "That is because I have this day cut off her head and driven a stake through her heart!"

"Good God!" exclaimed Ewan, horror-stricken.

"And I made a funeral pyre—of mountain ash—and her body lies on it, even now, surrounded by cleansing flames."

"Dale! And then you will be healed, also?" asked Bessie's anxious, eager voice.

Dale nodded affirmatively.

Ewan's eyes followed that movement of the doctor's hand to his neck; saw the two tiny punctures on his neck; the smeared dried blood which Dale had not yet stopped to cleanse from his skin, the remaining trace of Gretel's horrid feasting.

"You—you were bitten too!" said Ewan, and he walked all at once to the doctor's side. "Then what I heard last night—and saw—was not—my God, it was not a dream!"

He flung one arm about the fainting man, and supported him to the canoe, letting him slip down upon the bundles packed into the little craft. "Forgive me, old man. I—I couldn't understand," he murmured. Horror glazed his eyes.

"Let's get out of here," he said sharply. "Bessie, I'd rather wait to eat until we're downstream a bit. How about it, sis?"

"Ewan, you're beginning to understand!" she agreed, gladly. "No, I'm not hungry. I—I just want to get away."

"Understand?" whispered her brother, his face chalky with the bizarre thoughts he dared not permit organization in his mind. "Bessie, I don't want to understand! I only know that I want to leave this place just as quickly as I can."

"And you realize that Dale—?"

"Poor chap! Jove, Bessie, let's get busy. I—I feel as if I couldn't breathe freely here," Ewan declared, setting his sister an example by emptying the hot water from the kettle, wrapping the kettle in newspapers, and grabbing up the plates that she had been setting out for that last lunch.

It did not seem ten minutes before the scurrying feet had made those last trips back and forth between cabin and canoe. Bessie got in, lifted the doctor's head upon her lap, and saw with lighter heart that he was breathing more easily. Ewan lifted his paddle, dipped it into the water, and pushed against the sandy bank to set the canoe afloat for the trip downstream.

Dale opened his eyes suddenly, staring about him as the branches overhead slipped backward when the stream took the canoe and drew it away from the shore.

"Stop!" he said feebly. "I cannot go yet."

Apprehension held Bessie silent. He added:

"I put fire to the funeral pyre, but until—everything—is consumed, I dare not go."

"How shall we know?" the girl queried, nervously.

The doctor's hand, in that significant gesture, went to his throat.

"When the last trace of her—it—has been consumed in the cleansing flames, these wounds will disappear, Bessie, for her spell will be broken."

Slowly the canoe drifted downstream. As it slipped between the green banks, signs of that portent which all three awaited came to them through the summer air. Flying bits of charred wood carried upward by the powerful draft drifted about. The smell of burning wood—and something else more pungent—assailed their nostrils. As they drew nearer the lodge, the reason for this was clear.

In front of the building, where the woods had been cleared away, there had been built up a funeral pyre of dry wood, upon which undoubtedly the doctor had poured gasoline to saturation, for the flames were glowing with a red heat about the central part of the pile. As now and then the flames and the curling smoke blew aside, they could see on the summit encircled by leaping fire, something—a dark something with a glint of gold—that would be—her hair.

As the trio stared, the center of the pile collapsed before their straining eyes, and that dark something crashed inward to the heart of the flames. The fire leaped higher, then died away into smoldering embers...

"It is over now," declared the doctor.

He closed his eyes, a kind of grateful relaxation in the tired drooping of the lids, and a quivering sigh of relief shook his body weakly. As one hand moved across his neck, a faint smile came to his pale lips. It seemed to Bessie that they had taken on a warmer tinge; that his waxen pallor was altering subtly to a more lifelike and natural hue.

"All right to get away from here?" asked Ewan gruffly, paddle lifted to send the canoe swiftly on its way downstream.

Bessie's eyes were swimming with thankful tears. She dipped her handkerchief into the brook's running water; gently cleansed the doctor's neck, wiping away the crimson stains. Ewan, as well as she, saw that the punctures were gone.

"Everything is all right," responded the girl, her voice trembling with an influx of happiness as she realized what this meant to Dale and to her.

The artist dipped his paddle into the sparkling water, as if his drained energies had been renewed miraculously.

The little craft slipped swiftly downstream toward civilization, sanity, clean, everyday life.

The fetters had been broken, at last.

The End

Other From Beyond Press Releases

This World Belongs to Us:
An Anthology of Horror Stories about Bugs

Twenty terrifying tales of the creepy-crawlies who were here before us and will be here long after we're gone. Featuring stories by Kealan Patrick Burke, Paula D. Ashe, Laurel Hightower, V. Castro, Felix I.D. Dimaro, and more.

Paperback:$13.99
Hardcover: $17.99

This Is Life: Rediscovered Short Fiction
by Frank London Brown

More than one hundred flash fiction pieces by the author of *Trumbull Park* offer poignant, vibrant vignettes of Black life in Chicago in the 1950s and early 1960s. Recently rediscovered and collected here for the first time ever. Introduction by Sandra Jackson-Opoku.

Paperback: $10.99

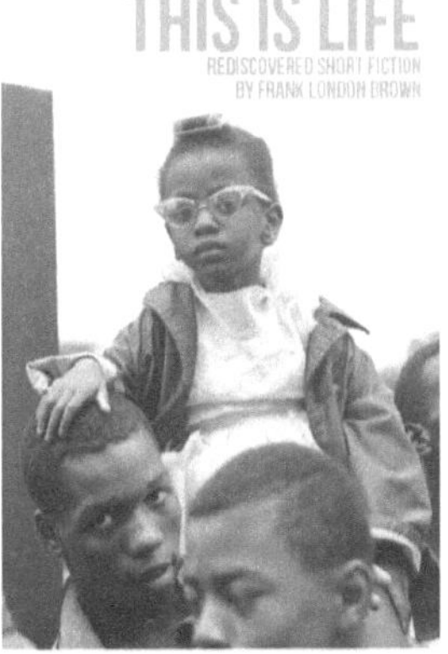

Escalators to Hell: Shopping Mall Horrors

Everyone's favorite suburban hangout becomes a site of unimaginable terror in twenty-one stories of one-stop shopping gone wrong. Featuring stories by Christi Nogle, Somto Ihezue, Angela Liu, J.A.W. McCarthy, Lor Gislason, Jennifer Lee Rossman, and more.

Publication date: February 2024
Paperback: $13.99

frombeyondpress.com